To Noah.

ADVENTURES
OF
RABBITMAN
SCOTT,
THE ADVENTURES OF
RABBITMAN

MARK WHIPPLE

Your friend

Cover by Paul Drake
Interior Illustrations by Paul Drake
and Karen Suisse

an
IAWriters.com
Publication

OTHER BOOKS BY MARK WHIPPLE

Pirates, Ghosts, Zombies
and other things that make me smile

Bizarre but True Tales
from the Twenty-third Dimension

Rabbitman II, the Second of Scott

Scott III, The Third Tale of Rabbitman
ALSO AVAILABLE:
Kosmic Karl (a feature film available on DVD)
Visit us at www.iawriters.com
and www.kosmicfilm.com

This book is a work of fiction. Names, characters, places, and incidents are either a product of the author's imagination or are used fictitiously, and any resemblance to actual persons, living or dead, (semi-or really-really dead), business establishments, events, or locales is entirely coincidental.

DEDICATED TO

Codename:
JJENKS, the most fine of all fine spy buddies.

PROLOGUE

*L*ight years away from the blue planet, the one some respectfully call Earth, a mighty war raged. A war so massive and all-encompassing, it was galactic in nature. A war so ~~big~~ that not only the survival of whole civilizations, but of whole planets, of whole solar systems and even of whole galaxies was threatened. This conflict, this battle, this war, this flaming altercation of cosmic proportions, this gigantic, galactic, universe-changing event came about because of a simple lack of communication.

CHAPTER 1
THE METHOD OF
COMMUNICATION

*F*ourteen-year-old Scott Mitchell, a tall, awkward boy with blond, slightly wavy hair and golf course green eyes. Today, like every other day, Scott walked home from school with his next door neighbor and pal, ten-year-old Jimmy Floyd Morristein. (Don't worry you won't be tested on his name since everyone who calls him anything just calls him 002— pronounced Double-Oh-Two.)

It had been an average day. Scott struggled to stay interested and awake…while somehow, Jimmy managed to love every minute of it.

"Well another day, another swift kick in

the head," said Scott.

"Yeah, I'll say," said Jimmy (002). He quickly followed with, "Wait, no. It was a great day. I didn't end up in a garbage can and I learned something new in every class. It was a very great day. Why it very well may have been the best day of my life. High five to myself." 002 jumped up and clapped his hands over his head.

"Ah, Jimmy if only I could grasp the thrill of learning like you do. I mean, like so what that a spider's butt is called an abdomen. A butt is a butt by any other name."

"Wait Scott. Look at that, you learned something today. Everyone thought you were asleep, but you were learning. Abdomen."

"Abdomen. Oh my," replied Scott, "I guess I did."
"Maybe you didn't mean to and maybe you didn't want to, but now you know something that will stick with you for the rest of your life."

"Maybe you're right, a spider's butt . . ."
"Abdomen."

"Yeah abdomen. A spider's abdomen has changed my entire view. Wait, it's more. It has changed my heart and has given me a whole new love for school."

"Scott, you're weird."

"I know. I'll see you tomorrow," said Scott as he cut across the lawn and headed towards his house.

"Yeah, see you, then," said Jimmy as he walked towards his home, three houses away.

Scott walked up the stairs of his porch, opened his front door and yelled, "Hey, Mom, I'm home!" Which actually means, *"Mom, I missed you, I'm glad to be back and I need some sort of acknowledgment that you're here and still love me."* This he had done and said nearly every day of his life when he came home from school. "Hey, Mom, I'm home!"

"You went off to school and forgot to feed your rabbit. I'm sure it's starving!" was her answer from another room. This was his mother's way of saying, *"I love you, too, but you have got to be more responsible. Now go feed your rabbit."* (I'm sorry for having to translate some of these common Earth phrases, but this book you are holding happens to be one of the most widely read works throughout the universe. Many cultures on many planets would not completely understand these simple phrases— not to mention mothers and boys sometimes don't really understand either)—however, in order to expedite this story, I will try to avoid translations where the statements aren't dramatically changed from their spoken meaning.

"No Mom, I'm sure I fed him before I left." Which is a boy's way of saying exactly that. Scott went to the refrigerator and took out a carrot, which was also something he had done nearly every day. Crazy? Yes, but Scott liked carrots.

"It didn't have any food or water when I went out there," his mother called from another room.

"He must have knocked over the bowls. I'll get him some more."

Scott took another bite of the carrot and headed out the door. He went to a bag of Faulty's Scientific Rabbit Chow, took from it a cupful of green pellets speckled with pink dots and walked to the rabbit's cage. In the cage was a rabbit—not just any rabbit, but a big-fluffy, black and white rabbit with one black ear, one white ear and pink eyes. All right, it was a lot like any other rabbit, except this rabbit had once won a red ribbon in the county fair.

Not only was this an award-winning rabbit, the rabbit was named after Scott's favorite grandfather (the one on his mother's side):

Jumpy. No one really had an explanation why Grandpa Jumpy was called Grandpa Jumpy, except that maybe it was because of a nervous condition he had. That was his name and Scott named his rabbit after him and loved his rabbit enough to feed it Faulty's Scientific Rabbit Chow, which was "guaranteed to make a rabbit jump higher, run faster and always have a sparkle in its eye."

"Hey, Jumpy, don't eat your food so fast. Try to make it last for the whole day," Scott said as he scratched the rabbit behind the ears. "If you'll space it out, then I won't have to come out here to feed you twice a day—and maybe my mom would mellow out."

The rabbit just stared at him. Scott petted the rabbit's head.

"You're still a good rabbit." Scott poured the pellets into a bowl and walked away. He returned with the garden hose and filled up the water dish. Scott took two more bites of his carrot and gave the rest to Jumpy.

Jumpy nibbled at the carrot.

Now, you probably believe this is where this amazing and mesmerizing story started, but it isn't. The story actually started many light years away from Scott and his hungry rabbit. You see, many light years away, there is a planet of beings called Verblockians.

Verblockians are more advanced than Earthlings in nearly every way. The Verblockians have spaceships that can fly so fast that they can actually arrive at destinations hours before they leave. They have buildings with no mounted foundations, which just hover in the air. Instead of vacuuming the carpets, they simply turn the buildings upside down, shake them hard, then turn the buildings on their sides and pour all the dirt out the windows. It only takes one person thirty- minutes to clean an average two-hundred story building.

For breakfast, the highly advanced Verblockians eat one small green pill a month, for lunch they eat one small blue pill every other month and for dinner they have pizza and ice-cream with chocolate toppings—or whatever else they could possibly want. This they eat every night. Yes indeed, Verblockians truly have an advanced civilization in every single way—every single way, that is, but one: their language.

Verblockianese, to us on Earth, wouldn't seem advanced at all. You see, their verbal communication is achieved by sticking their tongue out, closing their lips around it and blowing air from their mouth. To the untrained ear, their words sound like an Earthling giving another Earthling a "Raspberry". Now that I mention it, even to the trained ear it sounds exactly like that, too.

When speaking Verblockianese correctly, one must, as they say on Verblock, "Let the spit fly." Of course, on Earth, if we spit when we talk, it's embarrassing. Also on Earth, when you or I make the Verblockian sounds in our speech, or in any other way, we should always say, "Excuse me" or promptly blame someone else. But again, that same sound on Verblock, in a restaurant, will promptly cause the waiter to bring out a pizza and a large bowl of ice cream with chocolate topping.

I may sound somewhat critical of this language, but I don't mean to be. You must realize that this method of communication has served them well for centuries. Many wonderful and powerful speeches that inspired the Verblockians to greatness were delivered in this language. Of course, after such a speech, the speaker would always have to change his shirt because of the amount of slobber on it.

(AUTHOR'S NOTE: On Earth we sometimes call someone who talks a lot "long-winded". In Verblockianese they refer to someone who talks a lot as being "Pllbbpbppblbl," which, roughly translated, means "well-spitted," a very high and well-received compliment.)

Yes, this language had served them well—until they met representatives of the planet Sleesloock (pronounced with a major lisp). The Sleesloockians had perfected donuts and wanted to open up trade with the Verblockians, so a trade meeting was arranged. The Sleesloocks, who brought cases and cases and cases of their perfect donuts, were greeted by the Verblocks in their raspberry-blowing language. The Sleesloocks were offended. On planet Sleesloock, the second most offensive thing one could do is to give a Sleesloockian a raspberry. (The most offensive thing to do is to throw dog droppings in his hair. Much ruder. But still, a raspberry is extremely rude.)

Sleesloockianese was equally offensive to the Verblocks, for Sleesloocks do not use a verbal language at all (since they have no vocal cords), but instead communicate totally by wiggling their fingers while placing their thumbs onto different areas of their body, like ears, noses, chins, cheeks, foreheads, elbows and (for special emphasis) rear ends. Every single word in their language happened to be a very rude gesture to a Verblockian.

The donut negotiation lasted three days. The Verblocks stood on one side of the crates of perfect donuts and presented their best, most dignified and respectable raspberries. While on the other side of the donuts, the Sleesloocks were silent, with their thumbs planted on various areas of their anatomies while they wiggled their fingers. When the negotiations were over, the Verblockians not only didn't get any donuts, but found they were at war and had dog doodies in their hair.

As you may have already guessed, this war is widely known throughout the Universe as the Great Donut War.

CHAPTER 2
THE GREAT DONUT WAR

*T*he fighting had raged on for years; one side with raspberries, the other side with donuts and terribly rude gestures, both advanced in their technologies, both challenged in their communication. Neither wanted to fight. Both sought a truce, but whenever a peace negotiation was held, one or both parties ended up with dog trailings in their hair. The war continued. Which brings us to a small war vessel owned by the Verblockians in the middle of heavy fighting on the front lines of the war. (I should point out that with the advancement of technology, "the middle of heavy fighting" is somewhat misleading—you see, the closest the Verblocks ever came to the Sleesloocks in their war vessels was 500,000 miles away. But at that distance, with their advanced weapons, it would be compared to two enemy soldiers of Earth fighting, with bazookas, hand grenades, machine guns, tanks and missile launchers, while both are in the same foxhole. To be only 500,000 miles away was a horrifying position to find oneself during this battle. Pherrrrrbbble rays and Slobber knocker-bockers were flying all around them. They fought back with flbbbbbre and pppppppppss.) (I'm sorry, I cannot translate these weapons to Earth words because there are no weapons like them, real or imaginary, on Earth. In fact, even in Earth's best science fiction, these weapons are still in the experimental stages. Also, I must use the Verblockian name for each weapon, as the Sleesloocks' written language consists of small pictures of thumbs and waving fingers, and I don't have those keys on my keyboard.)

In the war vessel, lights flashed at stations and sirens sounded while blasts were exploding all around them.

The captain yelled, "phwwebbbphbbrrrbbber!"

A voice from the engine room called back,

"bbbbblerlllor!" (I'm sorry: I meant to keep this translated, but in the heat of battle, in the middle of a war, sometimes I get too excited and make mistakes.) Let's see, the captain said, "Frenchie, divert all power from the engine to the blasters."

A response came from the engine room: "Oui, Captain, but we can't divert much more! I'm afraid she'll blow if we try."

"Pleeebbbf, we must try or die," said the Captain.

"I'll get you your power, Captain," said Frenchie.

It was about this time that the Sleesloocks did the unthinkable and fired a FFLLPPLRR thirty thousand miles from the Verblock's war vessel. Again, if someone fired something at you on Earth and missed you by thirty-thousand miles, you would feel pretty fffbbfbbfllbbing lucky. But, with their technology as it is, thirty-thousand miles, was a direct hit. You see, a FFLLPPLRR when fired creates a FLEEPPPLL WAVE which rapidly transmorgaforms everything within seven million miles of it into a thick goo, which, ironically, is somewhat like the consistency of the jelly found in the middle of the Sleesloocks' fancy donuts. Planets, moons, stars, comets and small ships all instantly changed. A ship thirty thousand miles away would have about eight seconds before it would be hit by the FLEEPPPLL WAVE and be transmorgaformed.

"They fired a FFLLPPLRR," was all a crewman yelled. An alarm sounded and everyone moved quickly in different directions, as they all were trained to do. And when they stopped, they were all strapped into seats or wall harnesses. The Captain pressed a button at his command post. The ship whirred and phrooooomed and was gone.

And now our story is getting very close to where it really begins and actually gets very good. So stay with us.

CHAPTER 2.5
(WHAT? IT'S A HALF CHAPTER)

At Scott's house, seemingly not a lot had happened. But in all reality, a huge amount had taken place. For you see, Scott had brushed and flossed his teeth. (Yes, this is important and there will be a test on it later.) Then he got his pajamas on, went to his window and looked out at the night sky. (Now hold that thought.)

CHAPTER 3
THE STORY IS GETTING GOOD

On the Verblockian's war vessel, the Captain did what every Verblockian Captain should do when threatened to be turned into jelly: he warned his crew, who raced to their seats and wall harnesses and then he engaged the Megatron Light-Flinger. (It sounds more impressive in Verblockian—but nonetheless, it's still impressive.) The Megatron, as we'll call it, actually turns time inside-out and propels a ship 100,000 times the speed of light. The only problem with the Megatron is that at that speed it takes two to three years to calculate a completely safe course of flight. You see, traveling at that speed, coming in contact with a particle of space dust will knock a ship light years off-course. Space debris much larger than a ping-pong ball will completely disintegrate an entire ship. Therefore, a captain should never use this speed, except in an emergency bail-out situation. In such an emergency, the Captain would aim the ship into the darkest spot in the sky and hope for the best. This is what Captain Zok faced and this is what he did: he steered the ship toward the darkest spot in the cosmos and fired the Megatron.

It has been found that blasting blindly into space would sometimes work, because in space there is an awful lot of space. This time they were fortunate: They only hit a few small particles, which sent them off-course, but did not disintegrate them. When the ship came out of Megatron Light Fling, those on board were relieved to find themselves not transmorgaformed or disintegrated. The only real problem was that they were heading directly—still traveling at an incredible speed of more than eight times the speed of light— toward a mid-sized star and nearly every drop of their power had been used by the Megatron.

"Ship's status," called the Captain.

"We've nearly lost all force fields and 99.3 percent of the power to the engines."

"Emergency stations," cried the Captain.

Everyone went to their stations, pressed buttons and turned knobs and did whatever they could.

"Captain Zok, at our present course and speed," a technician yelled, "we will hit the star in approximately forty-five seconds."

"Pbbbbblbblbbbffffd," said the captain. (I'm sorry I can't translate all these words directly. I mean, I could, but your mother wouldn't let you read this book, so just let it stand as written—which is a much nicer way to say it on Earth, anyway.)

"Do we even have enough power to veer one way or another and miss the star?" asked the Captain.

The technician punched more buttons. "Perhaps we could avoid direct impact, but my calculations show the heat of the star will still melt the hull and we will all be toasted kippers before we can sing one verse of our national anthem. We won't make it, Captain."

"Then, as your Captain, I must say that you have all performed honorably, bravely and have shown much dignity. Since we shall all die soon, let us die as men and women of nobility and sophistication. With that said, I must change my shirt."

"Wait, Captain Zok, keep that shirt on! There is a small blue planet between us and the sun. It has an atmosphere. We're going to hit it, anyway—if we could get fifty-seven percent of our force field up, we could slow ourselves in the atmosphere and make an emergency landing," said a crewman.

"Our force field is regenerating," spat out a crewman.

"What is the force field at now?" shouted Captain Zok.

"Forty percent," called another crewman.

"Frenchie, reroute every bit of spare power and get another seventeen percent on the force field!" yelled the Captain.

"Oui, oui." (Pronounced *we we*.) "I can give you sixty percent force field," said Frenchie from the engine room.

"But Captain Zok," a crewman spoke up, "I must report that at fifty-seven percent force field, there is only a three-point-eight percent chance that we will survive the impact."

"What are our chances if the force field is at sixty percent?"

"Let me punch in the numbers." The crewman entered the numbers into his computer, "We would have a seven-point-two percent chance of survival."

"Frenchie, give all the power you can to the force fields," said the Captain. "Our chance of survival is not great, but that's better than no chance at all. Prepare to hit the blue planet!" commanded Captain Zok.

Nervous tension filled the control room as the blue planet grew larger and larger, filling the monitors completely.

It was at about this time that the ship's doctor, a short, almond-shaped, hairy-like-a-bear man, entered the control room. He held the pot of a man-eating plant. The plant had attached itself to the doctor's face and seemed to be biting his nose.

The doctor blurted out, "Bpppllbbbbffff, Zok, I'm a doctor, not a horticulturist!"

Everyone on the ship laughed at the doctor's predicament, then looked straight ahead and screamed as loud and as long as they could as the ship violently entered the atmosphere of the blue-planet, Earth.

———————————

Now, remember that Scott had just _____ and _____ his teeth, (I told you that there was going to be a test). He was looking up into the sky and exactly at the right time, but unfortunately, closed his eyes and thought about a girl with very blue eyes.

If you were among the lucky ones who were outside that evening and were looking up, (and not thinking about girls) you may have seen what looked like a falling star streak across the sky. If you were listening carefully, instead of making a wish, you would have heard the screams and shrieks of the crew members and of Captain Zok as the ship raced through the air and crash-landed directly into the pile of rabbit droppings directly under Jumpy's cage. It was a fortunate place to crash land, for you see the ship's force field was not above fifty percent and rabbit droppings provided a smelly, but soft and squishy landing.

From the pile under the rabbit cage hissed a green-glowing gas, which floated up and encircled the award-winning rabbit Jumpy. Jumpy sniffed the air twice, paused, then after a moment, sniffed it a third time, got a green-demon-ridden look in his eyes, then tipped over and laid on his side, motionless, as if he were dead.

I'll have you know that I did mention the Verblocks were small. Perhaps I didn't mention *how* small. The entire ship and crew were no more than six inches across. I didn't make a big deal about the size sooner because it didn't seem to matter at the time. Big or small doesn't matter much when everything and everyone around you is similar in size.

Speaking of small, if you were a worm or a fly near the pile of rabbit yuck, you may have heard the Captain call, "Damage report, Frenchie!" Then you would have heard the following:

"We lost just about everything. It will take at least two months to fix."

"We don't have two months: We are at war! I need everything working in two hours," shouted Captain Zok.

"It would take a miracle to have it done in two weeks, but for you, Captain, I can have it done in an hour and fifty-two minutes."

"You make me proud. Take to it."

"Oui, oui, Captain."

I perhaps should have mentioned earlier, Frenchie comes from the French province of Verblock and therefore speaks Verblockianese with a French accent, (they spit more with their noses higher in the air). "Oui, oui," of course, is French for "Yes, yes," and is pronounced similarly to "Wee, wee," which is what a young person does in his or her pants if he or she does not make it to the bathroom in time to make number one. Ah, the method of communication.

"Oui, oui, Captain."

"Good work, all of you," said Captain Zok, with a tired thankfulness in his voice. "Now I will change my shirt."

CHAPTER 4
THE GREAT STAGE BUNNY

We now go back into the real world, or the real world as it is when you haven't just crash landed your space vessel onto an alien planet, into a mountainous pile of rabbit poo, which happened to be a very real world for every person on board the Verblockian war vessel. (You should be grateful that you were not in the Verblockian exploration party, wearing your Sunday-best shoes.) Perhaps I shouldn't say "back in the real world" at all, but instead, back in Scott's real world. Scott's world consisted of Mr. Phillips (the drama teacher) and twenty kids who all awaited direction. The rehearsal of the school's production of *Hopping Down the Bunny Trail* was in progress.

"Hold it, everyone! Where's Peter? I can't have a production without my Peter Rabbit.

Peter, Peter Rabbit where are you? Where's that rabbit?" bellowed Mr. Phillips, nearly jumping up and down as he pulled a very angry face. "Where is my Peter Rabbit!"

A few of the kids laughed.

"What? Did I say something funny?" asked Mr. Phillips. (Sometimes kids get giggling and once they're giggling, if you don't watch out, you'll lose them for hours.)

Scott, our hero (or "protagonist" as all English teachers would call him), entered from the back of the auditorium.

"Peter, there you are, you naughty rabbit! Where have you been?" asked Mr. Phillips.

"Car problems," said Scott.

"Car problems," nearly shouted Mr. Phillips. "You're fourteen. What kind of car problems could you be having?"

"I couldn't find anyone with a car to give me a ride."

"Well, hop, hop . . . We mustn't dilly dally," instructed Mr. Phillips.

Scott walked up onto the stage. Stacy, a lovely young girl Scott's age, was there and looked very pretty. Sure, I could tell you she had deep blue eyes like wading pools and lovely waving auburn hair and that her clear complexion was like that of pears and jelly—

25

but kids don't like that kind of talk, so I'll just say that she was a babe—you know, kind of hot. She also had a role in the play. Stacy smiled at Scott as he came close.

"Hi, Scott." Stacy beamed at him. (I may have missed a lot in the translation, but I'm sure that the beaming and the "Hi, Scott," meant that she was carrying a flame for him.)

"Oh, hi, Stacy," said Scott, which of course was his way of saying, "Wow! You spoke to me and your blue eyes really sparkle and your face glows of pears and jelly and your lips glisten and, and, and . . ." Scott tripped and fell to the stage.

One of the boys called out, "Hey Scott, did you have a nice trip?"

"Last fall?" added another.

Some of the kids laughed. (Kids of that age can be so rude.)

As Scott got up from the stage, he answered, "It was a fine enough trip: you know the Ozarks. It rained nearly every day."

"We're not talking about a vacation. We're dissing you about tripping and falling," said the boy. "Nice trip? Last fall?"

"Dissing?" asked Scott.

"Come on, Scott. Dissing: it's short for disrespecting. Everyone's been saying it for years."

"Oh. *That* dissing," said Scott.

Jimmy (002) went to Scott. "Scott, we all drew straws and this is the last one left."

Scott looked. Jimmy held one straw in his hand. Scott took it.

"The long one—you lose!" said the 002. "You've got to do it."

"I don't want to tell him. You tell him."

"Yeah, right. I'm an extra. You're the star. You tell him—he'll listen to you," said Jimmy and then quickly left leaving Scott holding the long straw.

"All right, Peter, we're taking it from the third scene in the first act," called Mr. Phillips. "Do you remember your lines?"

Scott thought for a moment. "Yeah, but . . . Mr. Phillips, everyone wants me to ask you why we're doing this play?"

"What do you mean when you say why are we doing this play?" asked Mr. Phillips.

"Just why *this* play?"

"We're doing this play because it's brilliant."

"No, really: it's about talking bunnies and talking turtles. Everyone thinks it's kind of silly, especially since there's no swearing and no one gets killed. You know we are almost in high school."

"Scott, Scott, Scott, Scott, Scott," Mr.
Phillips said with a long sigh. "*Hopping Down the
Bunny Trail* is a beautifully well-written piece of
theater which metaphorically represents the
repressed slaves winning freedom from their
cruel and heartless owners—which of course is
a universal theme that all men must struggle if
they are to be free." Mr Phillips nearly said it
all in one breath.

"Maybe just a few small swear words. I
mean, couldn't one just accidently slip out
while someone is dying on stage?" Scott fell to
the stage. "I'm shot, I'm dying and frankly my
dear, I don't give a . . ."

Mr. Phillips quickly interrupted Scott.
"Don't you dare say it, Scott! This production
will not only be for your parents and your
family, but will also be produced for the
children's wing of the Saint Lona of Balona
Hospital. Those kids are very sick and it's a
wonderful thing we're doing for them. We
shan't expose their little ears to dirty mouths."

Everyone was quiet.

"But . . ."

"Not another word. We have a play to put
on." Mr. Phillips clapped his hands.

Scott shrugged his shoulders at 002, got up

from the floor of the stage and brushed himself off.

"All right, Peter, we're taking it from the third scene in the first act. Do you remember your lines?" Mr. Phillips asked.

"Yeah, I remember," Scott said confidently, then added a very weak, "I think."

"Then places, everybody," said Mr. Phillips. "Just start when you're ready, Peter."

Scott got into place.

"Okay, I'm ready." Scott took a moment to get into character. "Oh, please, Mr. Fox, don't put me in no stew, you know how I hates to be boiled with carrots and the likes."

"Hold it! Hold it! Cut, cut," interrupted Mr. Phillips. "Peter, we're starting at scene three of the first act."

"Wasn't that it?" asked Scott.

"Oh, you jest. Someone help him with his lines, people," Mr. Phillips said in a sing-singy voice.

Stacy offered, "Oh, Mrs. Frog, you're going to have a party tonight?" With a look of sincerity, understanding, and plums and jelly.

"Oh yeah. I know, now," Scott said. "Thanks Stacy." Again, Scott was thinking about her wading pool eyes and her glistening lips and . . . and . . .

"Then let's just start where we left off, from the first," Mr. Phillips interrupted.

"From the first of the play?" Scott asked.

"No, Peter. From the first of Scene Three, Act One," said Mr. Phillips.

Scott assumed his place on stage.

"Okay, I'm ready." Scott paused to get into character again. "Oh, Mrs. Frog, you're going to have a party tonight?" Scott said to a girl who, even without makeup, had something of a frog face. (And I say that in the nicest way— I mean a frog face wouldn't work on everyone, but she was working it, not in a hot way, but kind of a strong country girl frog face sort of way—okay, maybe I should shut up about it. In fact if you would be so kind as to forget that I even mentioned her frog face, I would be grateful.)

"That's right, Peter and it's going to be the biggest and the bestest party there ever was or ever could be and there will be food and you is invited," said the girl with the short, round face and mouth that went nearly from ear to ear. (And since it's not politically correct to mentioned that she could lick her eyes with her tongue, I not going to.)

"Boy, oh boy! That is my favorite kind of party," said Scott.

"What's your favorite kind of party?" asked the girl.

"One where there is food and where I is invited," Scott answered, happy with his delivery. He looked past the girl and looked at Stacy who was standing next to a tall oak tree made out of paper-mache. She was looking at him. Both smiled.

(Now, I could tell you all about the entire rehearsal and a few hundred other details and subtleties, but if I did, this book would have to be ten million pages long—I believe that just may be too much to carry in an average sized backpack. So with that said, I'm just going to skip straight to the end of the rehearsal.)

Stacy went to talk to Scott. I'm not going to mention her eyes like wading pools and the glow of her skin and her glistening lips, etc. I'm not going to mention any of that, even though Scott was thinking about all those things—still, I won't mention it. I won't mention those things at all.

After the rehearsal, Stacy went up and spoke to Scott. "I was wondering if you wouldn't mind walking me home tonight?"

"Oh. Of course I wouldn't mind," said Scott.

"That would be really nice of you," she

said, with an extra sparkle in her eye. "My parents are at a company party and my mom insisted that I find someone to walk home with. I mean if it wouldn't be too much trouble."

"No trouble at all. In fact it won't be nothing but fun. Sorry, I'm still talking like Peter Rabbit."

"It's alright, I like it," said Stacy with a smile. They left the theater and headed towards Stacy's home.

Scott was a little shy and felt awkward and found it hard to talk, realizing that this was the first time he had ever been alone with a girl, but as they walked it became easier to speak.

"It's a lovely night," said Stacy

"If you're wearing enough garlic to keep away the werewolves and vampires," Scott blurted out. Realizing that it sounded better in his head, than coming from his mouth. "You know it's a full moon."

"Are you wearing garlic," asked Stacy.

"No, do I smell bad?" asked Scott.

"No, no. You smell fine. It was just that werewolves, vampires and garlic statement."

"Yeah, I really don't know where that came from and how it got out of my mouth so quickly," said Scott. "I feel kind of stupid."

"Oh don't. I like werewolves and vampires. I mean in books."

"Yeah, in books, they're much better behaved. I mean, than in real life." Scott was feeling silly again.

It was about this time, when they arrived at Stacy's house. Scott walked her to the porch.

Stacy looked at him with her wading pool blue eyes and said, "I really appreciate you walking me home."

"Any time," Scott said. "I really enjoyed it."

"Me too," she said with her glistening red lips. Scott couldn't decide whether to look at her lips or to gaze into her eyes when she spoke. He found both made it hard to breathe properly. He thought about looking at the moon, then forgot and continued to gaze into her eyes.

(Any youngsters or youths or whatever you prefer to be called, [I'm talking to the little ones], who are reading this book may wish to skip to the end of this chapter because there's going to be some smooching and it isn't going to be pretty, [I mean unless you like that kind of stuff] and if I'm not mistaken, the smooching is starting right away—FLIP TO THE END OF THE CHAPTER NOW!)

I warned you and yet you're still reading. You stayed . . . but what do I know? Maybe you are ready for this kind of smoochie-face stuff. Now, there's nothing wrong with a guy gazing into a girl's wading pool eyes, basking in the glow of her skin and/or relishing the movement of her glistening red lips, but I just have to warn you when it's happening, it's never long before some smooching follows. So, with that said, I'll give you one last warning. RUN TO THE END OF THE CHAPTER! LAST CHANCE!

(You're still here, so I'll just tell it like it is.) There was an awkward moment of silence. Maybe Scott was thinking about his lines, or those lips, or those blue eyes, or if swamp monsters are found in this neighborhood or if he's supposed to open the door for her or one of a hundred other things, but he can't think of the right thing to say, or actually anything to say at all. Just then Stacy came close to him. Scott couldn't believe his good fortune: she smelled of lilacs or blueberries. He wasn't sure which one it was, but he liked it. Normally when someone entered Scott's space (the space around him within the reach of his arm), his natural inclination was to back away, but this time, for some reason, he didn't.

"You know, I think you're the best one in the play," she said.

"No, not me. I keep messing up my lines," he said, a little embarrassed.

"But you are really good when you *do* do your lines right."

"Thanks."

There was another awkward moment. Scott wasn't thinking about speaking at all, he was thinking of lilacs and blueberries, made into a pillow that he could hug and hold on to. Stacy leaned forward. Scott still couldn't believe his good luck. He also leaned forward awkwardly, but instead of the perfect kiss, his forehead slammed into Stacy's forehead.

They both backed off and rubbed their foreheads in surprise.

"Scott," Stacy said, "you hold still." She then leaned forward and kissed him.

"Wow! That was much better than the first try." Scott said, awkwardly. His heart was racing and then it felt like it stopped for an instant, but then it felt like it started again and everything was perfect . . .

"That was because you walked me home and because I wanted to."

"Well, what would you say if I had just walked you home and I just wanted to do this?" He leaned over and awkwardly kissed her back (not *on* her back, silly: He kissed her on her lips . . . kissed her back on the lips . . . oh, never mind). He actually missed a little and ended up kissing her just below her nose, but it was still pretty close so she didn't mind much, and he didn't notice.

"I would say that it would be all right," she said.

"Really?"

"Really."

"Stacy, I don't want you to take this the wrong way, but you're the best kisser that I've ever kissed and I'll tell you I've kissed quite a few."

"You've kissed quite a few?" she asked, a little surprised and a little hurt.

"I'll say. Three: My mom, my grandma and my great aunt May. That's my grandmother's sister. They've been living together for about forty years"

"And I'm the best kisser?" she asked with a smile.

"Of course, hands down. In fact, my great Aunt May and grandma nearly cured me of kissing forever. They made me want to be a monk. It was awful. Then they pinch your cheeks and say, 'Oh, he's grown so much, but he's still our little cutie-pie. Give us another kiss. Remember when we used to change his diapers?' Seriously, Stacy, your kiss was so much better—you really are the greatest."

"Oh, Scott." She hugged Scott then pulled away. "I'll see you tomorrow."

"Why, what's tomorrow?" asked Scott.

"School." She said with a smile.

"Oh yeah, thanks for reminding me."

Stacy went into her house. Scott stood on the porch for a moment. "Wow," he said as he touched his lips with his fingers, trying to find if the warmth of Stacy's lips was still on his. He wasn't sure, but he found if he closed his eyes, he could see her coming to him with those lips and he could almost feel the kiss from her again.

Scott fell off the porch.

(I warned you and warned you and warned you again about the smooching, and you continued to read and expose yourself to the kissing stuff. Oh my, oh my.)

CHAPTER 5
HOW RABBITMAN BECAME
RABBITMAN

Wow, we got out of that smooching stuff alive and relatively unscathed. Skipping forward to the next morning, Scott walked out of the house carrying a backpack that he used for school.

As he left, his mother called, "Scott, don't you forget to feed your rabbit." This of course was his mother's way of saying, "I love you, study hard and don't forget to feed your rabbit."

"I'm going to do it now, Mom." Which was Scott's way of saying, "I love you, too, Mom. Thanks for thinking about me and my rabbit."

Scott walked to the rabbit's cage. Jumpy was twice the size that he was the day before and had a wild look and a green glow in his eye.

"Oh my, Jumpy, you're huge," said Scott. "I told you not to eat your food so fast. Maybe I'd better quit giving you Faulty's Scientific Rabbit Chow."

As Scott put his hand into the cage to get the bowl, Jumpy jumped and with a huge spark, bit Scott in the fleshy part of his hand between his thumb and forefinger. The rabbit then jumped up and out of the cage and ran down the street, sparking with every third or fourth hop.

Scott watched the rabbit for a moment, got dizzy, and then blacked out.

Now, this chapter could end now and we could go directly to Chapter 6, "The Awakening," if it weren't for the fact that a lot of parents only let their children read one chapter in a book this good, each night. If your parents are some of those, and we quit here, then you would have to go to bed now. So to help the kids stay up and get excited about reading, and since Chapter 5 just started, I'm going to throw caution to the breeze and just keep on going. But of course, I'm going to have to pause a bit so everyone will have a chance to get their BBs stacked, or their ducks in a line, whichever may apply.

Let's see, in the last chapter (which I know happened to be the first of this chapter), we left Scott passed out on his lawn by the rabbit cage. And there he laid. Now close your eyes and imagine that you're Scott, hearing the voice of your neighbor, ten-year-old Jimmy, speaking.

"Scott! Scott? What are you doing asleep on your lawn? Is your mom mad at you?"

You can open your eyes now, because that's what Scott did. He wasn't sure where he was, or why he was where he was, so he didn't say anything and Jimmy just kept on talking.

"Scott...Scott...Scott, you all right?"

(If you haven't opened your eyes yet, it's a good time to do it now, so go ahead and open your eyes. . . . Oh PPLLLPPPLLP. It's no use. We've lost some of our readers. We'll just have to go on without them. I hope the rest of you will keep your eyes open at least until the end of the chapter.)

Scott woke up and opened his eyes—still dazed. "You're not my mom," were the first words he uttered.

"I know that. It's me: 002," said Jimmy.

"What am I doing out here on the lawn?" asked Scott.

"I don't know, Scott. It's your lawn. I just

found you here."

"What time is it?"

Jimmy looked at his watch. "It's 7:35 and 42 seconds . . . 43 seconds . . . 44 seconds . . . 45 seconds. We'd better hurry or we'll be late for school."

"Is today a school day?" asked Scott.

"Of course it is. Come on, or we'll be late."

"Hey look, someone left my school stuff out here. This will save some time." Scott picked up the backpack and started walking towards school.

"My alarm didn't go off and I didn't wake up until I had found that the cat had curled up on my face and I almost suffocated. We're really going to be late." said Jimmy anxiously.

"I gotta quit sleeping on the lawn—my neck hurts." Scott stretched his neck, then rubbed his hand where his rabbit had bitten him. "Ouch. My hand feels like something bit me." He looked at his hand. "Something *did* bite me."

"Let me look," Jimmy offered. He took Scott's hand and looked at it. There was a small bit of blood where the rabbit bit him and his whole hand glowed slightly green.

"Wow, it looks like a big old nasty deadly poisonous garden spider bite," offered Jimmy.

"The kind of garden spider that bites people who sleep on their lawn. You may die."

"I'm not going to die."

"I'll bet you do."

"Okay, if I don't die you give me ten dollars and if I do, I'll give you ten."

"It's a deal. Shake on it," said Jimmy.

"Deal," said Scott.

"A sucker's deal," smiled Jimmy.

"Like taking slobbery candy from a baby," said Scott.

They did a special handshake, which consisted of, among other things, locking thumbs and making their fingers fly like a bird, as spy-buddies sometimes do, and then both said, "Spy buddies forever."

"So, 002, how have you been doing?" asked Scott.

"Fine, but I wish I didn't have to be 002. I think it's a dumb spy-name."

"No, it's a great name for a spy. Think about it: It's five better than 007 and he happens to be somewhat of a celebrity," offered Scott.

"It's dumb. Everyone says I look like 'double-oh *number* 2'."

"No you don't. Not even a little bit. . . . Wait, what does double-oh *number* 2 look like?"

asked Scott.

Jimmy whispered to Scott.

"Oh, like *number two*?" asked Scott loudly. "No, no. You certainly don't look like *number two* at all. I'll find you another spy-name."

"It won't be easy. Good spy-names are hard to come by."

"How about Mad Dog Asparagus?" asked Scott.

"I like Mad Dog, but I think we'll have to lose the vegetable. Mad Dog is kind of phat."

"Then how about Mad Dog Artichoke? That's kind of phat, too. You know: phat like hot, not fat like 'Dude, don't sit on me—you'll make my eyes pop out.'"

"Scott, you're even weirder today than normal."

"That's 'cuz, I'm phat, too."

"Scott, I'm really worried about your spider bite. I may have to up my bet to twenty dollars."

"It's your money, Mad Dog Rutabaga."

"How about let's lose all the vegetables completely and my spy-name will just be Mad Dog."

"All right. Mad Dog it is. Phat, way phat. Mad dog is phat. Way phat. Why, you're the phattest of them all. Phattest of all the skinny kids."

Jimmy listened to Scott for a moment. "If that spider that bit you was radioactive and it doesn't kill you, or turn you into a mutant or something, then maybe it could turn you into a super-hero like Spiderman. His spider was radioactive," said Jimmy, "and your hand is kind of green like his was."

"Yeah, right. Wait it is green?" said Scott.

"Kind of a glowing green," said Jimmy.

"It's probably just a grass stain," Scott replied weakly.

(Probably? Probably not. The whole course of the planet—perhaps the course of the universe—was about to change forever as the boys headed off to school and we end this chapter so that the little ones can head off to bed. Nightie-night my young friends. Don't let the radioactive bed bugs or rabbits bite.)

Extra (for the truly committed reader):

Some of the more observant readers are saying, "Wait a minute. Jimmy is ten and Scott is fourteen, how come they are both walking to junior high school together?" That's a very good question and now is as good of a time as any to tell you the answer. Jimmy is an E. L. P.er. You see, he is a very bright young man and had skipped quite a few grades and had been placed in the program for very bright kids, called E. L. P., which meets at Scott's school. I believe E. L. P. stands for Extended Learning Program. Of course, the bigger students call the E. L. P'ers, Extra Little Pupils, which seems to work too.

CHAPTER 6
THE TOWER, THE PEG, OR
ATLAS' SPEAR

On the outskirts of Twin Pines there is a very strange and interesting rock formation. You see, to the east of Twin Pines there is a mountain. Not a huge mountain or even a large mountain, but a mountain just the same. (Because it is taller that one thousand, it qualifies as a mountain.) There is a road that scenically winds up a hill that leads to the mountain. At one point, the road comes very close to a cliff, (not so close that it would scare the drivers or their passengers, but close enough that one could view a strange and interesting land formation. You see, forty-seven and a half feet from the cliff, there is a huge pillar that rises five hundred and thirty-three feet from the bottom of the canyon. That is roughly equal to the height of the cliffs across from it. The top of the pillar is three hundred and twelve feet from side to side and is nearly perfectly round. Over the years, the people who lived in or near by Twin Pines called it many different names, which I won't go into now, but have alluded to in the title of this chapter—what I will go into is how this pillar has baffled geologists for years. You see, the lands in the surrounding area are limestone, conglomerates, sandstone and volcanic rock, but the pillar is solid granite. No one knows how this pillar was formed. The cliff across from it is made from a volcanic flow and is quite hard, but not nearly as hard or strong as granite. So over many, many centuries, the cliff and the surrounding area has eroded away, while the granite remains strong and tall. What has baffled scientists the most is that the nearest granite rock formation is over four-hundred miles away.

Now when your parents were little grass hoppers, an eccentric billionaire, (of course this was a while ago, when a billion dollars was a lot of money), bought the pillar and put in a drawbridge and moved a castle, one stone at a time from England and reassembled it on top of the pillar. This billionaire was a little cuckoo, (but because he was rich, people just called him eccentric). This billionaire insisted on having a moat around his castle, which there was no real reason to have because of the five-hundred foot drop on all sides of the pillar. He build his moat, filled it with crocodiles and all would have been fine except he had a very difficult time keeping water in it. You see for some reason unknown to him, the moat would leak, and not just in one place. So this poor billionaire would have to catch his crocodiles, put them in the dungeon of the castle and then he would have to struggle to find the leak. And then he had a battle to patch it. Then he would have to refill it with water and crocodiles. In a day or two, when it would leak somewhere else again, he would have to put the crocodiles in his dungeon and he would patch it, refill it, and then it would leak in a different place, and then he would have to start the whole process again: catching his crocodiles, putting them in the dungeon, patching the hole, refilling the mote with water and the crocodiles, and then the first place would leak again. Instead of just being a little cuckoo, he eventually went completely insane as he obsessed over the moat and the keeping it filled with water. The billionaire loaned his crocodiles to a zoo and put himself into an institution to help him rest and cope. And although he could have left at any time, he wound up spending the rest of his life there. (What can I say, he loved pizza days—they were Tuesdays and Fridays.)

The castle was left empty and fell into

disrepair. Over the years, different businessmen tried to save the castle. Someone turned it into a Hotel Bed and Breakfast, but found there wasn't enough traffic in Twin Pines to make it productive. Another tried to turn it into a museum, but didn't have enough interesting things in it to attract much of a crowd and there weren't many parking places.

The castle was finally abandoned and left empty for many, many, many years. And again, this all happened while your parents were still young.

CHAPTER 7
THE ANTAGONIST (THE BAD GUY)

*T*he castle sat vacant for many years until it was recently purchased by Lambert T. Houston. Lambert was an average size man who truly believed that he was smarter than everyone else in the world. Lambert loved the castle and loved the drawbridge and the mote, (but wondered why nobody thought to keep it full of water and crocodiles). He also loved the five hundred plus foot drop off that surrounded the entire castle. Lambert spent a small fortune on fixing the place up. He even filled the moat with water and wondered where he could get some crocodiles. (He didn't wonder long as the water had all leaked out of the moat.) He decided that he would fix it and fill it with water again and then find some sharp toothed reptiles. But he also decided that he would do it later since his mind was now occupied with something else.

Lambert T. Houston worked vigorously on a computer next to the television set which his girlfriend Barbara was watching. Barbara was a well curved woman with a huge pile of blond hair on top of her head. It is quite possible that Lambert was spending time with her because of her mind.

On the television was an anchorperson reporting the news.

"In science news, early this morning, a meteor burst through our atmosphere. This in itself isn't really newsworthy, but scientists feel that the strange weather patterns in outlying communities were somehow related to the meteor—and strange weather it was."

A second newsperson joined in. "Right you are, Tom. We have had rain in most of the northern regions, which has caught us all off guard. Forecasters had predicted sun and were completely surprised by this sudden storm front."

"The strangest part of the storm is that in Twin Pine City, where the meteor is presumed to have hit, it has been sunny, clear and beautiful."

"I guess it's safe to say, if another meteor decides to hit, let's hope it hits us." The news people chuckled as if a real side-splitter had been spewed.

"You don't know how right you are," Lambert muttered to himself as he continued to work at his computer. He turned off the TV and then typed on the computer. The computer screen brought up a picture of the world. Pressing a few more keys, he set a meteor in motion on his screen. The meteor went streaking into the world at a 47-degree angle. Where the meteor hit the atmosphere, the image stayed the same, but the surrounding areas started to change colors to black and blue.

"Ha, ha, that's it! I've proved it!" exclaimed Lambert.

Barbara sat on a couch a few feet away from Lambert, filing her fingernails. "What's *it*, dear?" Barbara asked.

"The weather changes were brought on by a highly-accelerated, positively-charged meteor striking through the atmosphere at an exact 47-degree descent."

Barbara laughed a little, then stopped. "What?" she asked with a blank stare.

"For some reason, the meteor was heavily charged. I can reproduce it! That means I can control the weather!" Lambert was excited.

"So?" asked Barbara, wanting to share in the excitement.

"The one who controls the weather, controls the world!" He laughed insanely.

"Oh. So . . . so . . . " she thought for a moment, then a small light (like you would find on the side of an electric toothbrush to show that it's being charged) clicked on in her head, "Oh! A . . . a . . . a . . . really?"

Lambert rolled his eyes, then continued his work while Barbara returned to her fingernails, and we come to the end of the chapter. And so we must say "Good night" to the younger kids who can only read one chapter per night.

CHAPTER 8
NEVER EAT THE MEATLOAF

*I*n the school cafeteria a most horrifying event was taking place. Very old women in hair nets were serving mass quantities of food, from a large slime covered scoop. It was casserole day and was made up largely of foods randomly found in the fridge. Food which wasn't quite old enough to toss, but wasn't fresh enough to be served without catsup. Many of these questionable foods were mixed into a huge bowl, slopped into huge cooking trays, covered with cheese and baked at three hundred and fifty degrees for two hours. The conglomerate was very unceremoniously called mystery casserole. And just between you and me, I think if the aliens, which had crash landed into the rabbit poo, had to choose between the casserole to crash into, or the rabbit poo, they would choose the poo. All right maybe I'm being too hard on the mystery casserole, but what can I say, the cheese toppings would gum up and ruin everything on the outside of the ship.

I'm sorry. I was just being silly, and just teasing the casserole and the school cafeteria. The kids looked forward to it and Scott actually liked it. (It usually had bits of carrots in it.)

At a table, Scott, Jimmy and Stacy were sitting with their lunch. Stacy was speaking

"Scott, I'm sure that I could teach you algebra," said Stacy

"Thanks for your confidence, but no one can teach me algebra."

"I could," said Stacy.

"Don't be so sure," interrupted Jimmy between mouthfuls of the questionable casserole. "He's . . . a . . . a . . . ."

Jimmy took too long, so Stacy jumped back in. "They have been able to teach horses and monkeys to do similar math. Why Jimmy is a fifth grader and he learned the math. I can teach Scott."

"I'm not a fifth-grader. I'm a ninth-grader just like you. The only difference is I skipped four years of grade school," said Jimmy in a very defensive way.

"I know. I'm just trying to make a point with Scott. He can learn math," said Stacy.

"People have different strengths and weaknesses," said Scott. "I'm with Mad Dog on this one. I don't think math is my strong point. I'm a. . . a . . . a . . . .You going to finish your casserole?"

"No have at it," said Stacy.

Scott picked up her plate and scraped the casserole onto his plate. "My mom thinks that I may be going through a growth spurt."

"Come to my house after school. I know I can teach you math," said Stacy.

"Can I come too?" said Jimmy with a casserole smile, (don't ask). "I would like to see you teach Scott Mitchell math."

"No, you'll just distract him. Scott, be at my house, alone, with a pencil and a piece of paper at exactly 4:30, and I promise I'll teach you math." said Stacy as she wrote a line into her day planner. She stood up. "Exactly 4:30."

"Okay," said Scott.

Stacy left the table. Scott watched her leave as Jimmy played with his Jello.

"I'm from outer space." He held the green Jello up to his eye and squished it between his fingers and said, "Doo doo doo doo dooo."

"That's nice," said Scott. "I'm going to

learn some math."

"Oh, I thought you were encouraging me and my alien impersonation."

"Oh no. Did you do an alien impersonation?"

"Yeah, it was pretty cool."

"Do it again."

"I can't I'm out of Jello."

"Bummer dude."

And the matter was left at that, and Scott had a math date.

CHAPTER 9
THE PROTAGONIST

On the alien space ship, (I know the name of the chapter is "The Protagonist," which, of course, means "the hero," or "the good guy," and everyone figures that it's Scott, who very well may be our hero, but I have to mention the Verblockians because they're largely responsible for our "hero" becoming a "hero"—so stop interrupting) . . . anyway, on the Verblockians' ship, everything seemed to be in working order. Everyone was at a station, pressing buttons, moving levers and turning knobs. There were no warning lights flashing and the Captain was wearing a dry shirt.

"Engine room, what's your status?" sprayed Captain Zok.

"Oui, Captain, we are capable of two-thirds power," said Frenchie.

"Let's hope that's enough, Frenchie," said the Captain.

"Oui, oui, Captain," replied Frenchie.

"Well then, hurry," the Captain said. "We'll wait."

"What?" Frenchie asked.

"I'll need you here when we take off. So, hurry and go to the wee-wee if you have to. It's going to be a long trip home at two-thirds power and I don't want to have to stop so you can go to the potty later," said the Captain.

"No Captain, 'Oui, oui,' as in, 'yes, yes.' You see, I have already gone wee-wee."

"Oh then, very good. Give me thrusters and all the lift we have."

"Oui, oui, again, Captain."

"I thought you already went."

"Oui, I did, and yes, yes, we can go now."

"Then make it so."

The ship made the groaning sound of a not-fully-functioning space craft as it began its thrust out of the hole.

It rose slowly.

The crew nervously watched and hoped, while the monitor showed the ship freeing itself from its prison of gigantic rabbit droppings.

As the ship rose, the first-mate addressed

the captain. "Captain, this is a most unusual planet. All sensors show that its surface is made up entirely of digested carrots, alfalfa and other vegetable products."

"What are you saying, in layman's terms?" asked the Captain.

"From all readings, this planet consists mainly of fecal matter," replied the first-mate.

As the ship rose, huge rabbit droppings could be seen through the monitors.

"Layman's terms!" shouted the Captain. "Layman's terms!"

"Poo, Captain. It's all poo and we landed right in it. Poo as far as our scanners will scan, which is not very far because they too are covered with poo. Nothing but poo. The whole planet, it's all poo. Plops, dukies, droppings, manure, ca-ca and do-do . . . everywhere, the whole planet is nothing but do-do," replied the first mate.

"Enough of the layman's terms," cried the Captain, "Now go wash your mouth out with soap."

The first mate left the bridge.

"Do-do, huh?" continued the captain.

The captain held up his finger and paused, as if he was going to say something profound and important. "Then," he said and paused for effect, "as soon as possible," another pause for more emphasis and more effect, "we had better get the ship washed."

Suddenly, one of the crew, who was working at his station, became worried, "Captain, we have a huge electromagnetic force closing in at an incredible speed."

"Condition Red! Full force field. Give me visual," sprayed the Captain.

The large screen in front of the crew was very unclear. It looked like a huge pair of blurred blue jeans coming towards them at an incredible speed. Of course, the image was blurred because of the poo that was on the ship's camera. Everyone on the ship was frozen in horror.

Now, let me point out that this "huge electromagnetic force" was just Scott, jogging toward the rabbit cage as the little ship was emerging from the droppings. The ship had a slight green glow around it, as did Scott, and as they came closer together, the glow of both increased in intensity. Scott stopped jogging and staggered, looking loopy as the glow grew brighter. He staggered and stumbled, continuing toward the rabbit's cage and the tiny spaceship. Small sparks started to fly between Scott and the spaceship. Scott staggered closer, when all at once, a huge green arc shot from the ship to Scott and from Scott to the ship.

The ship popped and smoked and fell back into the hole. Scott shook, staggered a few steps, then fell unconscious to the ground.

I won't ask you to close your eyes again, since we lost so many readers the last time. (It's nearly impossible to read with your eyes closed, and how are you supposed to know when to reopen them?) But that's neither here nor anywhere else, whereas Scott was there, and somewhere else again, on his lawn, with his eyes closed and out cold. Then he heard:

"Scott! Scott! Wake up!" This time, it was Stacy.

Scott opened his eyes to see her beautiful wading pool blue eyes and glistening lips.

"Oh Scott, you had me so worried!" Stacy held Scott's head on her lap and gently stroked the side of his face.

"Hi, Stacy." Scott was still loopy from the shock of the spaceship, or maybe from the wading pools of her eyes. "Where am I?"

"Your front lawn. You must have passed out. Are you okay?"

"I'm fine, I think. I had the craziest dream. I was like Superman. I had the cape and everything, except that the big red "S" wasn't on my suit, it was painted right on my chest. I couldn't fly and I was only wearing my underwear. The fate of the world rested in my hands and I'm in my underwear. It was really crazy." he said. Then he had a thought. "I got arrested."

"Scott, maybe we ought to get you to a doctor."

"It was you. You got me out of prison and brought me my pants, but they weren't regular pants, they had feet in them. You know, like little-kid pajamas. Now that I think about it, it was a rabbit suit, ears and everything."

"You must have hit your head."

"It was so real. I hate dreams like that. But you were very sweet. You liked me. Stacy, thanks for bringing me my clothes. Your lips . . ." He moved close to her as if he would kiss her. She let his head drop.

"You were supposed to be at my house an hour-and-a-half ago. I was worried about you and came all the way over here, and found you sleeping on the lawn, dreaming about saving the world in your underpants. I'll tell you what, you must have hit your head real hard if you think I still like you after you dogged me like that."

"You think I chose to save the world in my underwear? I told you, it was just a crazy dream."

"I don't care if you have crazy dreams. Just don't have me in them." She stormed away.

"Don't be mad. You were wearing your clothes." He watched her leave, then called, "Hey, how about if I come to your house and we could study tonight?"

She stopped and turned to him.

"Okay, but if you arrive one minute after eight, I'll have my dad shoot you as a trespasser. And I don't want to hear any more about you dreaming that you're saving the world in your underwear while you're sleeping on your lawn, when you should be at my house."

She whipped around and stormed away.

CHAPTER 10
LIGHTS OUT ON THE WAR VESSEL

On the Verblockian war vessel, every light was out and every computer was down. Smoke was rising from the consoles and it was dark.

The captain called out. "Damage report."

"We can't tell. Everything is down Captain," responded an engineer.

"Well, wouldn't that be some sort of a

damage report," asked the Captain.

"Well . . . maybe, it could be . . . but there is no way of knowing while everything is down," said the engineer.

"Engine room what's your status?" called the Captain.

There was no reply.

"Our ship's intercom is down," said the engineer.

"Well, why didn't you include that in your damage report?"

"I didn't realize it was, until it was tried and found to be not working."

"Well then, I guess I'll just sit here in the dark and do nothing until you get everything working."

And that is exactly what he did.

CHAPTER 11
SUPER-HERO POWERS

Scott was supposed to be at Stacy's house at eight. He arrived at a quarter-to and waited on the porch until the second hand on his clock hit eight o'clock, then rang the doorbell. I tell you: deep wading pool blue eyes have a funny effect on a boy—and I believe it may be even worse when a boy has just been bitten by a bunny that has been exposed to green radioactive space gases. So those of you who fear the kisser, skip right to the second half of the chapter and don't wait a moment longer. There will be a lot of little stars, like this,

*   *   *   *   *   *   *

when the kissing is done and it's safe to return.

Stacy opened the door and invited him in. Scott and Stacy went to the kitchen silently and sat at the kitchen table. She immediately opened a math book and put it between them. After staring at the book for a few minutes, Scott said, "Oh, Stacy, I really think you're…you're…swell." He paused for a moment. "I think if we studied like this every night, I could get an 'A' out of any class." He moved close to her as if he were going to get a kiss. She let him get close enough to feel his breath on her neck.

"Scott, keep your eyes on the book. We're here to study, and I'm still mad about you not showing up this afternoon."

"I'm sorry about that. I don't know what happened. It's all kind of a blur. But thanks for letting me come over. I really stink at math." He moved closer.

"You just have to practice it," she said. "It's really kind of fun if you make it a game."

"I like games." He gently sniffed at her ear.

"Scott," she giggled, "What are you doing? Stop that. It's math tonight." She pulled away from him and took a deep breath. "Now just think of math like a game."

"Yeah, a game," moaned Scott. "A cruel game, where cruel minds got together to make stupid rules, to make regular folks with average-size brains go insane."

"Now, Scott."

"No, really. Think about it. They never had insane asylums until after they invented math."

"Is that right?"

"It most certainly is."

"I'll have to take your word on that," said Stacy as she looked back to the math book.

"Stacy, all day long I've been thinking about walking you home last night and that kiss you gave me was really great."

"It was nice," she said with a small smile of remembrance. "The kiss you gave me back was nice too."

"How about just one more?" said Scott. "Then I'll be able to concentrate better."

"No, Scott," said Stacy. She paused and thought. "Well, maybe just a little one. If you promise it will help you concentrate better."

"Oh, it will," said Scott excitedly.

He moved closer to her and they kissed.

I don't know if the kiss made him concentrate any better, but I know that it made her think a little less clearly about math.

"Can you concentrate better now, Scott?" she asked, a little breathlessly.

"A little better. But I'm thinking I'm going to need about thirty-five more to really get my head clear."

"No way! We're here to do math," said

Stacy. "And I've made a new rule: only one kiss a night." She thought a moment. "Maybe two on a special occasion."

"It's a special occasion, could I have my second one now?"

"What's the special occasion?"

"Arbor Day."

"Oh, is it?"

"I think so."

"You're just saying that."

"No, I really think it's Arbor Day."

"Well then, okay. Just one more for the trees. Happy Arbor Day," said Stacy.

They kissed again. Stacy pulled away and looked at the math book.

"Wow, this is the best Arbor Day ever," Scott said. "May I have another one?"

"No, I think that's enough. Let's study."

"Just one more."

"No, we need to study."

"Kiss, please?" playfully begged Scott.

"No. Math please."

"Math's boring."

"It's not as boring as waiting for a black eye to go away." She held up her fist to show that she meant it.

"Yeah, you're right." Scott shook himself and looked at the math book. "Okay, I'll behave. I promise." He looked at Stacy. Her blue sweater really brought out the blue of her eyes. "Just one little kiss?" he asked.

"A little one?" asked Stacy.

"Yes, very tiny."

"Just a tiny little one, then I'll be able to study for sure."

They kissed again.

"Now let's study."

"That was nice, now how about just thirty-four more?" He closed his eyes and came at her again with puckered lips. This time, she jumped up from the chair. He followed her.

"Scott, you promised."

"I'm sorry, Stacy. It's just that I have this, like, uncontrollable urge to smooch with you."

"Scott, sit back at the table and read the chapter," she said adamantly.

"Oh, Stacy, don't talk so romantically. You're already driving me crazy enough as it is," said Scott with a look of hunger in his eyes.

"Get away, Scott, or you're going to get it."

"Oh, Stacy. Just one more kiss."

"One kiss. Yeah, sure. No way! It would be like seventy-eight. You're crazy tonight."

She moved to position the table between him and her, which was what any sensible girl would do when she's with a guy who's been bitten by a green-glowing rabbit. (Now that I think about it, which is what any sensible girl would do when she's with any guy at all.)

"Get away, Scott! I mean it! I used to think you were such a nice guy."

He followed her.

"Your mouth says no," he kept moving closer and closer and closer with his lips puckered. "But your . . ."

She wound up and hit him hard on the chin.

". . . fist says no too. Much louder and much harder." He fell to the floor. "Ah, to be old and out of love," Scott moaned.

"I'm sorry, Scott, I tried to warn you, but you're just too crazy tonight. I'm sorry if I hurt you."

"I think I'll be all right," said Scott.

"Will you?" she looked with concern at him as he lay on the floor.

"I think so. I just need a kiss to make me feel better."

She wasn't quite sure if he needed another smack or another smack, but you can be sure she still had a fist made, ready if a smack were needed.

*　　*　　*　　*　　*　　*　　*

Coast is clear: you can come back. You were kept from the smooching and all you missed was Stacy socking Scott on the chin—in a most unromantic way.

Scott was now alone, walking home, mumbling, somewhat confused, somewhat lonely and somewhat feeling sorry for himself.

"My rabbit ran away." Scott walked lazily. "School stinks." He walked some more and kicked a rock. As he walked, thoughts of his actions with Stacy set in. He realized that he hadn't behaved himself properly and it hurt. "I'll bet Stacy won't kiss me for at least a month and then it's only going to be a half of a peck and I've got a killer urge for a carrot."

Scott walked past a gang of street thugs, who were presently out of things to do to keep them occupied.

One thug, who happened to be the biggest, saw Scott and called out, "Hey, you! Do you got a license to be so ugly?"

Scott was thinking about Stacy and carrots, and didn't hear the thug or even knew he was there, so he didn't respond.

"Hey, I'm talking to you!" yelled the thug as the group moved closer to Scott.

"He's talking to you!" another added. His voice was much higher pitch than the first.

"I'm sorry, were you talking to me?" asked Scott as he realized someone else was there.

"I don't see anybody else around, so I must be talking to you," said the big thug and his gang chuckled as if he had just said something funny.

"Yeah," shouted the thug with the high pitch voice. "We don't see nobody else around."

"What was the question, again?" asked Scott.

"I said: 'Boy, you got a license for being so ugly?'"

"Ah, no. Sorry," said Scott. "It will be almost a year before I even get my learner's permit." His mind was elsewhere.

"I said, do you have a license for being so ugly?" yelled the thug.

"Oh, I thought you were talking about my driver's license." Scott chuckled. "No, I don't have a license for being ugly either."

"Well you better get one," shouted the thug.

All the thugs chuckled.

"Okay." Scott was so concerned about his other problems and his craving for a carrot, he didn't even realize the thugs were taunting him. He walked on. With a nod of the big thug's head, all the thugs started to follow Scott.

Again, the biggest thug called to Scott: "Hey, how about you and I doing some dancing, little boy?"

"Ah. Thanks, but no thanks. I have a girlfriend . . . well I mean, I *had* a girlfriend and I don't dance with guys," Scott answered, thinking about how good a big, cold carrot that had just been taken out of the fridge would be.

The thugs followed, more quickly and closer.

"Hey stupid," the big one said, as he caught up and pushed Scott. "I don't want to dance, I want to fight!" The big thug stood with his fists in the air to show that he was ready to fight.

Again, Scott wasn't thinking too clearly. In fact, he wasn't thinking at all when a slight green glow appeared in his eyes. "Oh. Why didn't you just say so?" said Scott...but it was more like the green glow talking. Scott jumped six feet into the air, spun his legs around and gave the thug a double rabbit kick to the head. Scott landed softly, sniffed the air and continued his walk, while only thinking about his many problems.

The big thug didn't fare so well. He stood there with a silly grin on his face, like he was lying on a beach in Hawaii, drinking sodas and eating corn chips. Then, he dropped to the ground like a sack of potatoes falling off a turnip truck.

As you are already aware, street thugs aren't known for their rocket-scientist approach to life—they saw what had happened to their fellow thug friend and leader, and one called out: "Hey! The boy just double-rabbit-kicked Pete in the head. Let's get him!"

The remaining five street thugs attacked Scott, fists up and ready to make donut jelly juice out of our hero. Scott wasn't expecting an attack, but something in him clicked and the green glow turned on and before a nursery school teacher could sing two lines of *Here Comes Peter Cotton Tail, Hopping Down the Bunny Trail,* all five of the street thugs were on the ground. The ones that weren't out cold were moaning. I tell you, Scott had bounced about, hopped, sprung and jumped, darted here and flung there. Zigged to the left, zagged to the right, front and back. All the time those feet of his were going in every direction: kick here, boot there, drop punt everywhere-else-and-a-half.

When Scott was done with the street thugs, he continued walking and talking to himself like none of it had ever happened at all.

"All right, what if I promise Stacy that I'll behave? And if I could quit sleeping on the lawn, I could pay more attention at school. Yeah. I could be better. That would answer almost all of my problems. Then again, my rabbit is lost and I still have this killer urge for a carrot."

Scott continued to walk and continued to mumble. The thugs continued to lie on the ground. One of the thugs that didn't get it as bad as the rest managed to ask a question. "Was that a freight train or a passenger train that hit us?" (I personally think it was a passenger train, and it was from Japan, because freight trains don't move that fast or kick that hard.) The thug closed his eyes and was gone to the world.

One of the other thugs answered him the best he could. "Momma, could I have some more jelly beans with my sauerkraut, please? Night-night. Love you, mom." Then he was out, like the rest of them.

CHAPTER 12
CLASS

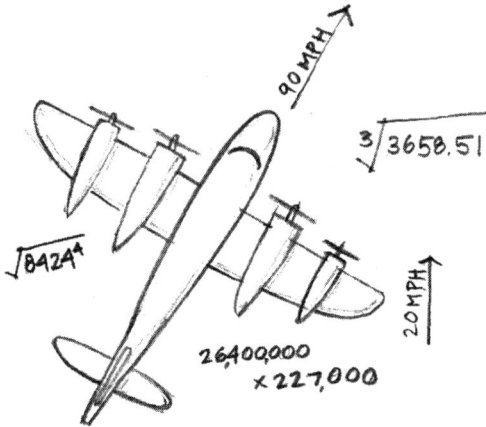

Scott showed up late for school the next day. He entered Mrs. Hommophelus's math class and noticed that everyone was at their desks working hard on a test. Jimmy was sitting towards the back of the classroom excitedly working on his test.

Scott saw Stacy and she saw him. She then looked down at the math test and would not look back at him.

"Scott, you chose to come late on a test day. Late on a one-third-of-your-grade test day." stated Mrs. Hommophelus, flatly.

"You didn't say we were having a test today," said Scott.

"I told you on the first day of class that we

would be having a test today," said Mrs. Hommophelus.

"And I was s'posed to remember?"

"No, I also told you and the entire class that we would have a test today, every day for the last two weeks."

"Really?" asked Scott.

"Yes, really, Scott. I know you weren't asleep every day."

"Dang!"

"At least you'll have the comfort of knowing that you failed this one without staying up all night uselessly cramming," Mrs. Hommophelus said as she held out the test. Scott reached for it as she dropped it to the floor.

"Oh, moted." said Scott.

"Good luck, Scott."

He bent down to pick up the test.

"Thanks. I'll need it."

"I know you will," said Mrs. Hommophelus. "It's one-third of your grade."

Scott walked to his seat. He looked around at the other students who were sweating over their tests and started to sweat himself.

"One-third of my grade!" Scott muttered.

He took his seat, looked for a pencil or a pen and couldn't find either. He tapped the student next to him.

"Scott, at least look at the questions before you resort to cheating," said Mrs. Hommophelus.

"I don't cheat. I need a pencil."

"I have extras. You may come and get one," said Mrs. Hommophelus.

He went back to the front of the class where Mrs. Hommophelus held a pencil. As he reached for it, she dropped it.

"Whoops," she said with an evil smile.

This time, with a slight green glow in his eye and lightning-quick reflexes, Scott snagged the pencil in mid-air before it could hit the ground. He went back to his desk.

Mrs. Hommophelus was amazed but didn't say anything.

He picked up the test. He looked at it, concerned. After a moment, he smiled and then quickly wrote on it. He looked at the second question, smiled and wrote.

"Cake," muttered Scott.

He flew through each question until he was completely done. Then he leaned back on his chair and started to occupy himself by making a dripping faucet sound with his mouth.

"Scott, both you and I know that you are

not done," interrupted Mrs. Hommophelus, "so quit trying to distract the other students. I don't grade on the curve."

"But I *am* done," said Scott.

"I like a good joke as well as the next, but we're having a test, Scott. Finish it!"

"I'm really done."

"Okay, Scott. Bring your test to me."

He took it to the front of the class and handed the test to the teacher. In a snooty way, she looked at it with a look that screamed that anything he had written must be wrong.

"Oh my. A miracle you got number one right!" She continued to look. "Two." She looked closer. "Three." She looked even closer, harder, almost frantically going through the test. "They're *all* right!"

Scott stood and smiled at Stacy, who was still trying to avoid him—even eye contact. He was very proud of himself.

"I was watching you the whole time, so tell me Scott, how did you cheat?" asked Mrs. Hommophelus.

"I didn't cheat," said Scott. "I just answered the questions."

"Then why didn't you work out the problems on the paper?"

"I didn't have to. I just worked them out in

my head."

"You can't work these out in your head," said Mrs. Hommophelus.

"I did."

Mrs. Hommophelus wasn't buying it. "Class, stop your tests for a moment. Scott believes that he has finished the test by working out the problems in his head in two minutes." She looked directly at Scott and asked, "Now, Scott, what is the square root of 8424 to the fourth power?"

"Seventy million, nine hundred sixty-three thousand, seven hundred and seventy-six," answered Scott.

Mrs. Hommophelus wrote on a piece of paper and punched numbers into a calculator.

"Just a minute, Scott." She continued to calculate, then, after a moment she exclaimed. "Oh my, you're right! How did you do that?"

"Just did it," answered Scott. He smiled.

"What's the cube root of 3658.51?" she asked.

"15.4087738837," he answered.

Mrs. Hommophelus worked on this question for a moment, then said, "My calculator only goes to nine digits. But the nine I have is what you had. Wow! That's amazing!"

"I know. Sometimes I even astonish

myself. And I didn't even study a bit. Well, actually I did study a bit." He looked at Stacy. "Best studying I've ever done." He smiled at Stacy, who quickly turned those wading pool blues in another direction.

"Why didn't you do this all year?" questioned Mrs. Hommophelus.

"I don't know. Guess I just didn't have my heart in it."

All of the students were interested and couldn't believe what they saw.

Jimmy looked into a math book.

"Hey Scott," Jimmy called, as he read from the book. "A pilot has been flying for an hour with his plane headed northeast, and learns from a weather broadcast that the wind has been blowing from the direction of 280 degrees at twenty miles per hour. The air speed of the plane is 90 miles per hour. In what direction has the plane actually flown and what is its ground speed?"

"The course was 54 degrees and the plane's ground speed was a hundred and two miles per hour."

"Jimmy looked up the answer in the back of the book. "That is so cool."

Another student shouted. "What's 26,400,000 times 227,000?"

The bell rang.

"Five trillion, nine hundred and ninety-two billion, eight hundred million," answered Scott.

Stacy grabbed her stuff, hurried past the teacher's desk, placed her test on it, and hurried out the door.

"Bring your tests up," said Mrs. Hommophelus. "Scott, I need to speak with you. You and I are about to make teaching history."

Scott didn't want to miss Stacy, and she was already out the door.

"I can't, I've got to get to gym. Coach said he'd unscrew my head and stick dog droppings down my windpipe if I'm ever late again." Scott darted out of the room.

"But wait!" called Mrs. Hommophelus. It was too late. He was already gone.

Scott rushed out into the hall. The hall was filled with students. Stacy walked down the hall, trying to hurry.

Scott looked one way, then the other. He saw her and started to run around people to catch up with her.

"Stacy, I'm sorry about last night. I wasn't myself. Can we still be friends?"

She looked as if she may give in, then was unsure.

"I don't know, Scott. You acted like you were crazy. I'm going to need some time to think about it."

"Yeah, I'm sorry. How about if after rehearsal tonight we go get some ice cream."

She started to soften. "Well, maybe."

"Then we could go back to your house and kiss some more."

"No!" She turned and stormed away.

"What, you don't want the ice cream?" Scott called.

She didn't answer him as she hurried down the hall.

(One would think that with all those math smarts and all those superhuman rabbit powers, he would have known better than to mention any of that kissing stuff in front of Stacy.) Scott looked at his watch and then hurried toward the gymnasium. He wasn't kidding when he told Mrs. Hommophelus that the coach didn't want him late again.

CHAPTER 13
THE BIG GAME OR THE GEEK TEAM

*T*he coach was a big and mean teacher with somewhat sadistic tendencies. (He liked to see people suffer.) He had a large cranium (the storage container for brains, usually kept on the upper end of one's neck—sometimes formally called the head or informally called a Brainium-Cranium). The coach used his large cranium more for knocking holes in walls, opening doors and smashing aluminum cans than for storing facts and quotes.

On the football field, he stood in front of the class of boys and spoke. "All right, ladies," (there were no girls or women present), "as you all know, football season is in progress. So, in honor of football, today we're going to try something different. This is how we're going to split up the teams: I want all the big, tough, mean guys on one team." He pointed to his right. "And I want all the little geeky guys to be on the other team." He pointed to his left. "Come on, let's move it, already!"

He blew a whistle and everybody hurried to get into the right team.

Scott went to the big guy team, even though he was shorter and much skinnier than the rest.

"Hold it, Mitchell! Wrong team," said the coach.

"No way! I'm four inches taller than any of them."

"Well I know that, Mitchell; that's why I made you quarterback and geek team captain. You see, although you're a bit bigger than the rest, you're still a little too little and geeky for my taste," said the coach.

"I don't know how to be a quarterback," said Scott.

"Oh, it's really easy. They hike you the ball and then before the big guys can catch and pound you into the ground, you make a touchdown. You can either run or pass or punt. For health reasons, I'd suggest you punt every time you get it." The coach then yelled to everyone, "We'll be using the scoreboard, so you'll all know how you're doing."

As the two teams walked to their sides of the field, Jimmy spoke with Scott. "You know Scott, the coach is missing the whole reason we have football."

"How's that?" asked Scott.

"You see, football was invented by little guys like us to get the big guys like them to beat each other up for a while."

"Really?"

"Yeah: quite ingenious. While they're beating each other up, they forget to beat *us* up. Think about it. Someone has figured out how to get two-hundred-and-fifty-pound guys, fifty yards apart, to run at full speed directly into each other, and they like it. It's quite amazing."

"I never thought of it like that before," Scott said.

"Yeah, it's great. The only way one could improve on football would be to get them to use sticks—no, bats! No, *clubs* to hit each other with. Yes, clubs. Then I would watch football," Jimmy said in a matter-of-fact way. Then he had another thought. "Just for kicks, you could give them one point for knocking out an opponent and after the opponent is out, they could score two more if they could knock themselves out."

The coach blew the whistle and yelled, "Okay, big guys. Kick the ball to the geeks.

As one can imagine, the big guys were big and the little guys were little and they were both lined up on opposite sides of the field.

"The reason we're doing this little object lesson," shouted the coach as he paced back and forth, "is that you all have the choice of what you want to be in life: little and geeky or big and strong. It's your decision. I'm just giving you guys a little help to think about it. Okay, start that clock. Let the game begin." He blew the whistle again.

The clock had started to tick when one of the big guys looked at the others and shouted, "Let's kill 'em." They all seemed to be in agreement.

The big guys lined up, placed a football on the tee and kicked it. As the ball flew toward the little guys, all of the big guys ran ferociously down the field.

Most of the little guys saw them coming and scurried out of their way. Jimmy tried to catch the ball, but dropped it. He picked it back up and saw that all the big guys were almost on him. He threw it to another little guy, who also saw the big guys. This little guy threw the ball up as high as he could then curled into a ball on the ground. The football landed in Scott's hands.

Scott froze, with his mouth wide open, as he saw the big guys advancing. His gum fell out of his mouth. Other than that, he just stood there, scared and motionless—kind of like a rabbit caught in the headlights of an oncoming semi-truck. Here came a huge wall of big guys headed straight for Scott—two of the biggest, angling in on him, one from the right, one from the left.

The coach watched and seemed happy with a big grin on his face.

It didn't look good for Scott, but his nose twitched and he got a slight green glow in his eyes. Just as two big guys dove in to make a Scott sandwich out of him, Scott leaped six-and-a-half feet straight up in the air. The two big guys met with a hard crash, right in the place where he was. When Scott came down, he started to run like a rabbit, weaving in and out, over, under and through, all while the big guys were leaping and diving where Scott had been, or at least where they thought he should have been.

Scott ran all the way down the field and made a touchdown.

The coach quit smiling and threw his hat

on the ground disgusted.

The score board flashed GEEKS 7—BIG GUYS 0.

"That was just lucky," yelled the coach. "Go ahead geeks, kick it to the big guys."

Jimmy went up to Scott. "You know, I think we could beat these guys. Next to us, they seem to be rather slow."

"Yeah, they're slow, but you do realize that if they catch us we're bug juice on the proverbial windshield of life," said Scott in a nervous tone.

"Oh yeah, I forgot about that for a minute," said Jimmy.

The coach blew his whistle again. Scott kicked the ball. It flew over the heads of the big guys, through the uprights and over the fence. The coach was amazed by the kick and had a hard time admitting it. "Nice kick," he said, very softly so no one could hear.

"Thanks Coach." Apparently Scott did hear him.

"Okay, big guys: take the ball on the twenty." He threw them a new ball.

The big guys lined up in a huddle. A big guy that must have been the quarterback spoke: "All right, here's the plan. I'll hit you," he pointed to another, "on the right side; you run it in for a touchdown. If any of the gum-wads get in your way, take them with you. Hike it on five." They broke from the huddle and all went up to the line.

"Fifteen right, left seven, five," said the quarterback, and the ball was hiked to him. The little guys tried to rush in, but the big guys just stood there and they couldn't get around them.

The coach stood on the side and smiled.

The quarterback threw the ball to an open receiver. The ball sailed through the air. No one was near the receiver. It looked as if it would be an easy touchdown.

In a flash, Scott darted across the field, jumped high into the air, tipped the ball away from the receiver and then grabbed it before it hit the ground. No one could believe it. Scott then darted left, right and with a few more rabbit moves, he took the ball to the goal for a touchdown.

The score board flashed GEEKS 14— BIG GUYS 0.

The coach again threw his hat on the ground.

All the little guys ran up and congratulated Scott. The big guys were mad and doubled their efforts to get the little guys, especially

Scott. They leaped harder, dove harder, lunged harder, kicked harder and swore more, but it didn't seem to help.

The game went on and on. The big guys got madder and madder, but there wasn't much they could do about it. GEEKS 21—BIG GUYS 0. Scott was just too fast. GEEKS 28—BIG GUYS 0. You would think the big guys could just hike it and run a power play to the right or left side and score a touchdown, but when they hiked the ball, Scott would dart in or leap over and take it out of the air before the quarterback could even get it. Scott would then run it in for a touchdown. GEEKS 35—BIG GUYS 0. They couldn't throw any passes that he couldn't intercept and take back for a touchdown. GEEKS 42—BIG GUYS 0. And you know what? It wasn't all Scott. Well, it was *mostly* all Scott, but all the little guys started to play with some confidence. Scott threw a pass to Jimmy, who caught it in the end-zone and made a touchdown. GEEKS 49—BIG GUYS 0.

The coach wasn't any happier than the big guys. It seemed his object lesson wasn't going exactly according to his plan.

When the bell rang, the score read 56 to 0. All of the little guys ran happily towards the locker room, cheering.

"Mitchell, I want to talk to you!" shouted the coach.

"Me?" asked Scott, as he went to the coach.

"Scott, I noticed that you have a small quantity of natural talent in the area of football," said the coach. "With my help, I think we could turn it into something special. I know it's late in the season, but I'm thinking I may let you sign up for the team. I think I could make you a star."

"Thanks coach, but I don't think so. I never really cared for the game. It's kind of silly, don't you think? Big guys beating each other up for points?" Scott nodded to the coach, "Well, got to go, coach." He ran towards the locker room, fresh, as though he hadn't even been playing football.

The biggest of the big guys led the rest of the big guys up to the coach. Most were limping. All were tired and covered with grass stains and mud. "Coach, we didn't understand at first, but now we think your point was well made, about us having the choice of being big strong guys or little geekie guys, we all talked about it like you said and we decided that we all want to be little geekie guys." He nodded, as did everyone behind him in humble approval.

The coach didn't know what to say for a moment, then he just screamed, "Ahhhhhh," for a very long time. After a while he gained some control and said in a much calmer, more disappointed voice, "Go shower, boys."

CHAPTER 14
ON WITH LIFE

*S*tacy was mad at Scott, but everyone else started to see him a little differently.

For example, a lot of people were in the hall when Susan, a pretty cheerleader, whose locker was next to Stacy's locker, and two other cheerleaders, met Stacy at her locker. "Stacy, how come you don't like Scott anymore?" Susan asked.

"Because he's crazy." Stacy said sincerely.

"Well, sure, he's schizophrenic, paranoid and suffers from a multiple personality disorder, but the three of you make a lovely couple," said Susan. The other cheerleaders giggled.

"You always hated him; why are you sticking up for him now?" asked Stacy.

"I didn't know that he was a math genius," she said. "They're the ones that become rich. I read a book all about it. I just think you'd better think about it before you dump him too hard."

"You've read a book?" Stacy asked.

"All right, it was on TV, but they were reading from a book. But think about it. Bill

Gates: geek, math genius, richest man in the world."

They closed their lockers and walked down the hall.

"I hear he can play football too," Susan said.

"Bill Gates," replied Stacy.

"No, Scott," giggled Susan.

"I don't know about that," said Stacy.

(They weren't the only ones who started to see Scott a little differently—Let's see, Mrs. Hommophelus, the Coach and everyone, the big guys and the little guys in gym class, not to mention the street thugs.) (I'm sorry. I said not to mention the street thugs, then I went right ahead and mentioned them—what kind of punk am I? Now in my own defense, I don't think it's so much of me being a punk, as it is a mistake in our society's phraseology. You see, quiet often one will say "Not to mention the time you did this or that and then they have to mention that time, so you will know the time that they are not mentioning. It's really quite bazaar if you think about it.)

As for Scott, life was pretty much the same as it had always been. He was at home lying on his bed, reading a comic book about a gang of super-mutant-space heroes, when a small red light mounted near his window flashed twice, then paused and then flashed three more times.

Scott pushed a button near his bed. A weight tied to a rope dropped from the ceiling and opened the window. In came Jimmy. Scott's bedroom is on the second floor, above the front porch. For Jimmy to come into the widow, he would have to climb the tree next to Scott's house, shimmy across a long branch, hang off the branch, then drop a few inches to the roof above the porch.

(I hate to do this, but marketing tests have shown that on some planets in the Universe, we have been losing readers in the eight to ten-year-old girls' category and the reason is that I didn't really mention how handsome young Jimmy is. Sure, I said Jimmy was smart, but the eight to ten-year-old-girls aren't thrilled by smarts, they seem to be only into looks. Of course, we've kept all the boys' attention with Stacy's deep blue wading pool eyes and all of the older girls are interested in Scott, especially now that they've found he can do math and play football. In fact, everyone is covered except the eight to ten-year-old girls. So in order to keep their interest, I need to tell you [eight to ten-year-old girls] just how handsome this young man really is. Here goes: Jimmy is handsome. He has two ears, two eyes and one nose with two nostrils, all approximately where they are supposed to be, and a mop of hair like a shrubbery. Most believe that the rest of his body will one day grow to match the size of his ears. (If that doesn't perk up the ten-year-old girls' attention, I don't know what will.) Oh, and by the way, he's smart too. (The new marketing tests are just in—we've got the eight to ten-year-old girls back—they love him. And who wouldn't. He's like a funny little troll doll…oops, we just lost the eight to ten-year-old girls again. I meant, troll doll—in a good way.)

And without further adieu, Jimmy, that handsome young man—two ears, two eyes, a mop of hair like a shrubbery, etc., came through the window.

"Scott! It's an emergency! I was in the store today and some guy bought a bunch of stuff including a high energy multi-packer frequency oscillator ion-charging atom fuser," Jimmy said excitedly.

"So?" Scott hardly even looked up from his comic book.

"*A high-energy multi-packer frequency oscillator ion-charging atom fuser,*" said Jimmy again, with a little more emphasis on every word.

Scott put down the comic book. "I think you mentioned that, didn't you?"

"He's planning something big," said Jimmy.

"Who is?"

"The guy who bought the stuff. I think he's going to try to take over the world."

"Why would he want to do that?" Scott asked.

"'Cuz, that's what crazy people do. They take over the world."

"No," said Scott. "Crazy people wear hats made out of newspaper, hang around by the malls and yell at the cars as they drive by."

"Well, yeah, some crazy people do that. Other crazy people try to take over the world," said Jimmy.

"You gotta be reading too much. Jimmy, I would suggest you spend more time watching TV," said Scott.

"After he bought the stuff, I followed him home, which wasn't easy, since I was on my bike and he was driving some crazy car—like crazy people drive before they take over the world. It may be a Volvo."

"Okay, I'm telling your mom that you're not watching enough TV and that you're eating way too much sugar."

Jimmy ignored him and continued his story. "He lives in that huge castle at the top of Vine Road. The one that was moved from England one stone at a time. It has a drawbridge."

"That place is crazy. Wait, it's a castle. Does it have a moat?"

"Yeah, but there's no water in it."

"No water?" asked Scott again.

"No water in the moat, already!" Jimmy almost shouted.

"Then I don't think we need to worry. It is generally accepted that you have to have water in the moat that surrounds your castle before you can take over the world."

"Scott, I'm really serious."

"What makes you think he's going to take over the world just because he buys a multi-atom whatever? Maybe he bought it for *good*. I mean, what's one used for?"

Jimmy went to the phone. He dialed a number that he had written on his hand and then hit the speaker button.

A voice on the phone answered, "Hello, Majorly Big Electronic Parts R Us. Jed speaking."

"Ah, yes, Jed," said Jimmy, "Would you

mind telling me what a high-energy multi-packer frequency oscillator ion-charging atom fuser is used for?"

"Well, I would say mostly for taking over the world and stuff like that," said the voice on the phone. "Hey, are you that kid that was in the shop today?"

"No." said Jimmy trying to make his voice sound lower. "I'm some old guy. Bye," he quickly hung up the phone.

"Who did you get to say that?" asked Scott.

"That was the guy at the store," said Jimmy. "You could call him yourself."

"Let's just say he wants to take over the world and he's going to do it with his multi-whatever-packer. What do you think we are supposed to do?"

"We lie low. Stake out his house and see if anything weird starts happening."

"How are we going to stake out a castle that was built on the top of Atlas' Spear?"

"Just a little up the road from the castle, there is a grassy spot just lower than the cliff. There are some rocks and some cover we could hide behind."

"Man, you've really thought his out. So, okay, when should we start saving the world?"

"Tomorrow, after school." Jimmy looked at his watch. "I have to go home for dinner now."

"Then I guess I'll see you tomorrow," said Scott.

Both went to the window.

"Spy-buddies forever," they both said as they did their spy-buddy handshake. Jimmy went out the window then poked his head back in. "See you tomorrow. Bring some snacks."

CHAPTER 15
LIGHTS ON

On the Verblockian war vessel. The computers had been down and the lights had been off for a very long time. The crew used flashlights (alien technology) that stuck to their noses, as they tried to repair the vessel.

They had worked long and hard hours and finally the lights came back on. With a cheer, (I'm not going to say what the cheer sounded like—remember they communicated with raspberry sounds, and everyone on the ship doing it as loud as they could at the same time would sound like five elephants at the zoo breaking wind in unison—therefore, I will not say what that cheer sounded like.)

So the lights came on. Everyone cheered and the captain was getting ready to spray some spit (make a speech), when there was a pop, some smoke and the lights went off again.

"Plllbbbbllblllbblblllppp," muttered the captain, which is a common response when something like that happens on his planet.

CHAPTER 16
THE PERFORMER

As you know, Scott was in a stage play, and if you are ever in a stage play, you will know you're going to have to rehearse and rehearse and rehearse and then rehearse some more. And that was exactly what Scott was doing in the center of the stage of the school's auditorium. The teacher, Mr. Phillips, was looking on, mouthing the words as Scott delivered his lines. "Yonder breaketh carrot patch, which calleth me to dine. A carrot is a gift from God, a gift of love divine."

"No, no, Peter: more feeling!" said Mr. Phillips. "You need to feel the love ensuing from the rabbit which is in you."

"I thought I was doing pretty good. I've even been eating all kinds of carrots," said Scott. "I'm really feeling this part."

Mr. Phillips, being the drama teacher that he is, went into elaborate motions and spoke as a Shakespearean actor. "'Yonder breaketh carrot patch, which calleth me to dine. A carrot is a gift from God, a gift of love divine.' Feel it, Peter! The yearning, the desire...he wants those carrots more than a rabbit wants love and you know how much rabbits want love." The other students giggled.

"Really? More than love?" asked Scott.

"Yes, much more. It's a carrot, you are a rabbit. You want it much, much more. Now let me see your 'yonder breaketh carrot patch,' again."

"Well, okay." Scott paused to get into character, then stopped. "More than love?" he said to himself. Then he spoke to the audience, "Yonder breaketh carrot patch, which calleth me to dine. A carrot is a gift from God, a gift of love divine." This time Scott felt it and delivered it...and it was perfect.

Mr. Phillips clapped and wiped a tear from his eye. "Yes! Yes! Never have I seen such a moment in all of theater. Yes, Peter! You felt it! I felt it! Thank you. We're done tonight. I'll see you all tomorrow evening." He continued to clap.

All through the rehearsal, Stacy avoided Scott. Every time Scott tried to speak to her, she would turn and head in another direction. With the rehearsal over, Scott knew it was now or never. He went to Stacy and spoke.

"I'm sorry, Stacy. Let's be friends." He could tell that she wasn't buying it. "I'll control myself. Trust me."

"I wouldn't trust you if you got a note from the Pope," said Stacy.

"Okay, we don't have to go out. Let's just talk on occasion and maybe sometimes you could give me a ride to school or somewhere—you know, like friends would do." Scott looked as if he was in more control than he had been in the past.

"Just rides and talking and that's it?" she asked.

"And we can be friends again."

"All right, friends again. Do you need a ride home tonight?"

"Well, I brought my bike, but I've been riding it so much lately that I'm starting to get a rash."

"We can put the bike in the trunk."

"Friends again?"

"Friends again. If you behave."

"Oh, I will."

They walked away together.

And he behaved himself all the way home.

*Now, if you have been paying attention you will have noticed that Stacy is driving and

Scott is not. An astute reader of this literary masterpiece will want to know if Scott is carrying a flame for an older woman. The answer is "no," well actually "yes," but she's not much older, four and a half months. She only has a learner's permit to drive, which only allows her to drive with an adult or to drive to and from school or on official school business, (which the play qualifies).

CHAPTER 17
THE GUYS IN BLACK SUITS

*T*he next day in class, you knew there were going to be some happenings and happenings there were.

In Mrs. Hommophelus' math class, Mrs. Hommophelus was anxiously waiting for Scott. All the other kids were already in the classroom. There were two men in dark suits waiting, one tall and one short, both wearing dark glasses.

"He's an inspiration," said Mrs. Hommophelus. "Lately he has been coming late, but he's amazing and well worth the wait."

"I just hope you're right and he doesn't decide to keep us waiting too long," said one of the men.

Scott entered the classroom. All the

students applauded. Scott looked around, wondering why they were applauding.

"Scott, I'm so glad that you are here today," said Mrs. Hommophelus. "I have two very special guests from the President's Foundation for Geniuses. They'll be testing your IQ to see if you qualify for an early scholarship and entrance into any of the Ivy League Schools. I'm sure you'll pass."

"I don't want to go to college yet. All my friends are here." He looked at Stacy. She gave him a nice smile and with her deep blue wading pools eyes looking beautiful and all, he really didn't want to leave.

"Scott, with your brain, you could finish any college program in a few weeks," offered Mrs. Hommophelus.

The tall man spoke. "Young man, you may have a special gift. We are here to see that you use it wisely. We have some math questions that we would like you to answer."

The short man spoke in a businesslike way. "Question one: The sum of the squares of .7321 and 5.113."

Scott immediately knew the right answer, but I don't know if he wanted to give it to the men.

"Ah, oh," he thought out loud. He looked

at Stacy, whom he would lose if he were sent off to college. "Eighteen," he said with a smile.

Mrs. Hommophelus smiled as if it must be the right answer. The short man shook his head ever so slightly. So slightly that only the other man notice that he had. "Question two: What is the square root of 1745.75?"

"One hundred and twenty-five thousand." Scott answered much faster.

The tall man spoke. "Scott, maybe you'd like to figure some of these out on paper."

"No thanks; I always figure them out in my head."

The short man spoke again. "Question three: If a hen-and-a-half can lay an egg-and-a-half in a day-and-a-half, how many eggs can five hens lay in thirty-five years. Do not forget to calculate for leap year."

The students watched anxiously.

"Twenty-two thousand seven hundred and twelve."

Now if you wanted me to, I could go on and tell you all the answers and the corresponding questions that went with them, but let's just call it good enough. I will mentioned, that those men asked and asked and asked. As for Scott, well, he answered and answered and answered. By the end of the class most of the students were asleep. The ones not asleep were occupying themselves by combing their hair, chewing gum, drawing on the desk, etc. Mrs. Hommophelus was not only thrilled to see the happenings, she loved it. Oh, how she loved it. She loved the spectacle, the drama and the pathos the men brought to her math emporium. The questions the men had asked had taken up nearly the entire class time. Scott still stood at the front of the class.

"Three and 15/16ths," came another answer.

The short man spoke again. "Question number three hundred and fifty two, the last question of our test. Calculate the area of a sphere with an external radius of 320.65 meters."

"That would have to be exactly 1,000 feet."

The bell rang. Scott was as ready to go as the rest of the class.

"Wow, saved by the bell," said Scott. "I'll see you tomorrow." With that, he got up and bounded out of the room. The rest of the class vacated the class with equal energy.

Mrs. Hommophelus was anxious to hear the results. "He's impressive, isn't he?" she asked.

"I'll say he is! Zero out of three hundred and fifty-two questions! He missed every one," said the short man.

Mrs. Hommophelus was stunned.

The tall man spoke. "But that in itself is impressive. The theory is that with the multiple choice section of the test, if the same test is given to a chimp, with proper motivation and a number two pencil, he will get eight to ten percent right. Yet your Scott scored zero."

Mrs. Hommophelus didn't hear much more, because she had started to mumble, "I will kill him. I swear, I will kill him." She had a look in her eye that made me believe she would.

"Have a good day, Mrs. Hommophelus," the tall man said and they both left the room. Mrs. Hommophelus continued to mumble the same thing over and over.

In the gym's locker room Scott dressed next to Jimmy.

"Hey, Scott how did you miss all the answers on that test?" asked Jimmy.

"I didn't miss them, I just multiplied or divided all the answers by pi," said Scott.

"Why did you do that?"

"I'm way too young to go to college. Besides, if I were a genius, guys like that would want to take a core sample of my brain, like they're going to want to take from yours," Scott said.

"Good point," said Jimmy.

On the football field, everyone stood around the coach.

The Coach spoke. "Yesterday we witnessed something which was nothing short of miraculous. I, myself, am now committed to becoming a church-going man. I'll be starting next week. And I owe it all to Scott, the best football player that I've ever seen," said the coach. Then he paused for a moment, sighed and continued . . . "Who incidentally told me that he is not interested in playing football for the team, which would be the best that I have ever coached and probably the best team there ever was or ever could be. So, today here's how we're splitting up teams. I want everyone on one team and Scott you're on the other.

"Everyone on one team? And Scott on the other?" one of the big guys asked. "That's not really fair, is it?"

"No, but I want you guys to try really hard anyway," said the coach. "Now I want everyone—except Scott—to head down there." He pointed to the far end of the field. Everyone headed down the field.

The scoreboard read SCOTT 0, EVERYONE ELSE 0.

"I don't really think this is a good idea," said Scott.

"I've got your butt . . ."

"Abdomen, coach."

"What!" shouted the coach.

"Abdomen, it's a nicer way to say butt. Well at least it is for insects," said Scott.

The coach looked as if his head was going to explode. "Mitchell, for fifty minutes a day, I got your butt, and I'll do with it as I see fit until you sign up for the team. Okay, let's get going."

Well, you know the picture: everyone headed to one end of the field and Scott stayed on the other. They kicked the ball to Scott. Scott got the green glow in his eye, his nose twitched, then he snatched the ball out of the air and ran around, through and over everyone. Then he scored a touchdown. I guess they weren't going for extra points, but he could have easily snapped the ball, held it, then kicked the field goal.

One side of the scoreboard got hot that day. It flashed SCOTT 7, EVERYONE ELSE

0, then there was a few plays and the scoreboard read SCOTT 14, EVERYONE ELSE 0, soon, SCOTT 21, EVERYONE ELSE 0, then SCOTT 49 EVERYONE ELSE 0.

When the bell rang, Scott trotted off the field. Everyone else was tired, hurt and spread all over the field. Scott went right by the coach.

"Scott, I know this is highly inappropriate, but I will give you money if you will play for me," said the Coach.

"You know, Coach, that wouldn't be right."

Scott trotted toward the locker room.

"I'll give you a car. A new house with a pool," shouted the coach. "You want a piano? I'll get you two. Puppies! You want puppies? I'll get you a hundred of them. You'll play on my team, Scott; you just wait and see! I'll get you, Scott Mitchell," the coach yelled, then grabbed his chest and fell over moaning.

CHAPTER 18
SPY-STUFF

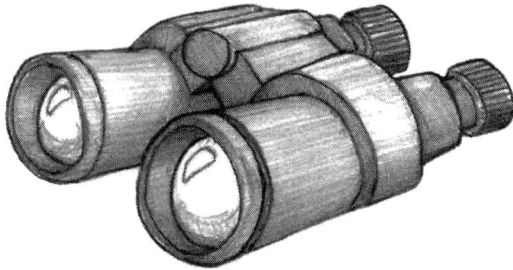

*J*immy and Scott had an appointment that day after school to do some spy-stuff, and that is exactly what they were doing. Spy-stuff. You see, Jimmy had binoculars and was spying from a green grassy area that was hidden near the cliff across from the castle. Scott's idea of spy-stuff was lying on his back with his eyes closed while he enjoyed the warm sunshine on his face. Their bikes were deposited on the grass not far from them. (You're saying, "Here are two boys doing spy-stuff and some writer had to bring up their bikes?" Well, I'm sorry, but it's important to mention the bikes for future reference.)

"I don't know if this is the best place to be," Jimmy said. "I wish we could get closer."

"Any closer and we fall to our deaths," said Scott, without opening his eyes.

"Don't be dumb. 'I wish we could get

closer,' comma, without falling to our deaths, period. It was implied."

"Well, you might have said that," Scott replied, his eyes still closed.

Without any warning, black storm clouds started to build. Immediately, the wind picked up and blew hard—blowing hardest directly around the castle.

"Does it seem to be getting colder to you?" asked Scott.

"Yeah, crazy. It's like it's going to rain or something," said Jimmy.

"Maybe we'd better go home before we get wet."

The wind continued to increase around them. It looked as if it was going to be a huge storm.

"I guess we could just do some more spy-stuff tomorrow," said Jimmy.

Scott started to put their things in a backpack.

"We did do pretty good," said Scott. "No one took over the world today."

The storm was getting wild...crazy wild. The wind blew so hard that Scott and Jimmy both squatted down and braced themselves between the cliff and a large boulder. Rain came down sideways and upwards, with drops so big they hurt when they hit. During this outrageous wind and storm, a man came out at the top of one of the towers and looked at the storm.

Jimmy saw him. "Look, he's there. Hide!"

They both crouched down further behind the large boulder, but kept their heads out so they could still see the man at the top of the castle.

"He doesn't look like he's the kind of guy that would take over the world to me," said Scott, shouting over the sound of the storm.

On top of the castle stood Lambert T. Houston enjoying the storm. It was raining so hard that water was filling the moat, wind was whipping and lightning was striking all around them.

"Yes! Yes!" yelled Lambert as he threw his arms in the air and danced around in a crazy way. (As crazy as the guys who wear newspaper hats and hang down at the mall, yelling at the cars that drive by.) He was clearly excited by this storm. He licked his finger, then held it in the air—like you would to check the direction of the wind. As he held his wet finger high in the air, a huge bolt of lightning struck it. The lighting lit Lambert like a light bulb for a moment, then he fell out of sight."

Scott and Jimmy gasped, looking at each other and then back at the castle.

Lambert popped right back up into view. His hair was sticking straight up and his whole body was soot covered and smoking. "I like it!" Lambert yelled, then laughed an insane laugh, threw his arms in the air, did another little dance and ran back into the castle just in time as another lightning bolt hit the top of the castle.

Scott and Jimmy saw it all. Both sat there with their mouths open, like they were trying to catch flies. Neither knew what to say and neither felt a need to say anything.

After a long moment, Jimmy spoke. "Did you see that?" he asked weakly.

"Yeah, did you?" answered Scott.

"I think so. What did you see?"

Unable to look away, they continued to stare at the castle and the storm surrounding it.

"A guy came out, licked his finger, held it in the air and was struck by lightning. Jumps up, yells like he liked it, dances around and went back in, laughing," said Scott.

"That's what I saw, too."

"Was that the guy who bought the multi-packer thingy?"

"Yeah. I think we should go to the cops,"

said Jimmy.

"I'll say we should," said Scott.

They still sat there with their mouths open for a long time and I could take a while to describe it and their eventual bike ride in the rain to the police station and stuff, but I'm not going to. I'm just heading directly to the police station. You see, it's your humble author's ability to jump and skip the slow parts, then jump right back in that has made this book such a huge inter-galactic success.

At the police station, Scott and Jimmy stood on one side of a huge counter and a large beef-cake of a Police Captain named Penski sat on the other.

Penski was talking. "I'm sorry, boys, but in our town, I don't believe it's against the law to be struck by lightning."

"But what about being crazy?"

"You can be as crazy as you want if you don't hurt or bother anyone. In fact, right now we have people down in front of the mall wearing hats made out of newspaper, yelling at cars as they drive by and you don't see them getting arrested."

"How about taking over the world?" asked Jimmy.

That caught Penski's attention. "Now *that's*

against the law. If you catch him taking over the world, you come and report it to me. I'll give that boy a ticket that he won't soon forget."

Jimmy wanted to say something and Scott knew that Jimmy wanted to say something, so Scott spoke up first.

"Well, thank you, officer," said Scott.

"That's what I'm here for."

Putting a hand over Jimmy's mouth, Scott grabbed his arm and escorted Jimmy from the police station.

Outside, the rain had stopped. The sun was shining and it looked like a beautiful day.

"Why didn't you let me say something to that cop?"

"I had a dream I was arrested, in that same police station. I was thinking, if I let you talk, the dream would have come true," said Scott.

"Well, the police are not going to help us at all. We're going to have to do it on our own," said Jimmy.

"We've got to wait and catch him doing something wrong," said Scott.

"Look: it's sunny again," Jimmy observed. "Should we go back?"

"I can't. I've got a doctor's appointment. My mom thinks that I may have something."

"Really? Like what?" asked Jimmy.

"A tapeworm, scabies or something."

"Really why?" asked Jimmy.

"Lately I've been eating all my vegetables," said Scott a little embarrassed.

"You're kidding," replied Jimmy with a tone of shock in his voice.

"No and it's crazy. They taste really good," said Scott.

"Wow! You may have something," said Jimmy. "I just may collect that twenty dollars. You're eating vegetables."

"Don't I know it. That's why I'm going to the doctor without a fight."

They both got on their bikes and started to ride.

"What's really crazy is that I feel fine," said Scott.

"Boy oh boy, I'll tell you what: I would never eat all my vegetables even if someone paid me."

They came to an intersection. Jimmy went straight and Scott turned to the right.

"I'll see you later," said Scott.

"I guess we'll just have to save the world tomorrow after school," called Jimmy.

CHAPTER 19
THE DOCTOR'S OFFICE

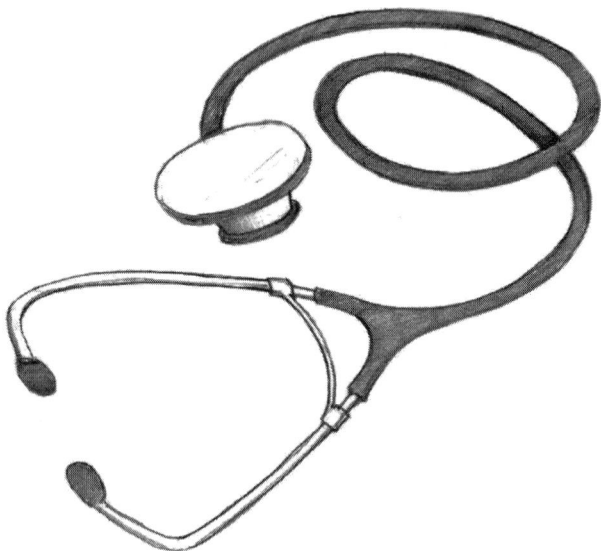

Well, those of you who only get to read one chapter a night are going to be disappointed tonight, because this is one short chapter.

At the doctor's office, Scott was sitting on a table wearing only a hospital gown, completely bored. The doctor came in. (For the marketing people of this book, I could say that the doctor was handsome and had the nicest bow in his back and legs, so we could keep our over-a-hundred-years-old women interested, but we're just going to have to accept the fact that this book cannot satisfy every reader in the universe.)

"Well Scott, I'm sorry to keep you waiting," the doctor said as he looked through his trifocal glasses at the clipboard he was holding.

"No problem. I like doctors' offices and sitting around in these gowns with my backside hanging out," said Scott.

"Great, then let's get started. Stand so your toes are touching this red line," said the doctor dryly.

Scott's attempt at sarcastic humor was completely wasted on this doctor.

Scott got up and stood with his toes on the red line.

"Read the chart, right, Doc?" asked Scott.

"No, *left* to right," said the doctor.

"Left to right?" asked Scott.

"Right-o," said the doctor

"Which toe?" asked Scott.

"Just read the chart, keeping behind the line!" said the doctor.

Scott started to read.

"A."

"A, E."

"R, G, C, D, A."

"M, F, G, R, T, U, S."

"B, G, D, F, H, U, S, B, X, C, R, Z"

The doctor was amazed. Scott continued,

"L, O, U, B, I, R, P."

"Z, G, A, T, H, B, L, O."

"EDMOND'S EYE CHART MADE IN USA, Copyright 1943."

The doctor was totally amazed. He walked quickly to the eye chart and looked closely, straining his eyes and his trifocals.

"Oh my, it is an Edmond's Eye Chart. I can't believe it," said the doctor. "You have at least 2000/20 vision. You can see clearly in 2000 feet what the average person would see in 20 feet."

The doctor read the eye chart, straining his eyes at the very bottom. "Copyright 1943. I'll be. This is amazing! You're going to make some optical history." He started writing on his doctor's pad.

"I memorized the chart," said Scott.

"You what?" asked the doctor.

"While I was waiting, which was like an hour, I memorized the chart. Pretty funny, huh?" Scott's humor was again wasted on the doctor.

"No, it's not funny at all," said the doctor.

"Maybe just a little bit?" asked Scott.

"Not at all. So how far can you read from there?"

"'Bout the fourth line."

"Then your vision is fine." The doctor wrote on his pad and left the office.

"So, what? I mean, that's the last of the tests; I can go now, right? Hey, where are my clothes?"

While looking for his clothes, Scott looked at the chart again. His nose twitched and his eyes got the green glow.

"Oh my, Edmond's Eye Chart . . .1943" said Scott. "Wait, Doc, I can read it to the bottom."

But the doctor was gone.

CHAPTER 20
THE SUBSTITUTE

*B*ack at school, class was in progress, but there was no Mrs. Hommophelus. There was a substitute teacher instead. The substitute was nice and everything, and if there was any fear of losing our seventy-two-year-and-older men, I would describe her baby-blue cat-eyed-bifocals and her beautiful white teeth that she soaks in a jar of bleach at night, the thick seam line up the back of her calf-high nylons. . . . (I guess we're just going to have to lose some of our audience sometime, because too much talk of such beauty amongst the elderly could make one lose his lunch.) Anyway, the substitute teacher was standing in front of the class.

"Your regular teacher," the substitute announced, "Mrs. Hommophelus, is receiving care and will not be with us. For the next few days I will be your substitute."

"Receiving care? What kind of care?" asked a concerned student.

"Professional," the substitute answered.

"Like professional yard care and painting?" asked a boy from the back of the classroom, who was drawing war planes and parachutes on the cover of his notebook.

"No, professional health care."

"Is she sick?" called another student.

"Yes, she is."

"Is she at the hospital?" asked a kind and caring student. "Maybe we should visit her?"

"Yes, she's at the hospital and no, we can't visit her. They don't allow visitors."

"What are you talking about?" called the boy with the parachutes and war planes on his note book. "I had my appendix out. They said it was so infected and full of pus that it was the size of a cantaloupe. They said it could have blown up and killed me and anyone who was standing within ten feet of me. They let me have visitors."

"Mrs. Hommophelus is in a different kind of hospital."

"We're in Twin Pine, there's only one street light and one hospital," said a girl from the front.

"No, there are two hospitals," said the substitute. "She has been committed to Twin Pine Sanitarium." She whispered when she said the word 'sanitarium' and hoped no one would bring up this subject again.

One student called out loudly, "Sanitarium? You mean the nut farm?"

The substitute was surprised and nearly tipped over by such a comment. "We do not call it a . . ." she paused and whispered "nut farm."

"The looney bin?" called another student.

"No," said the substitute.

"The cuckoo-nest?"

"No."

"The banana patch?" called another student.

"No."

"The peanut plantation?"

"No. We call it the sanitarium, and there she is receiving professional help. It's nothing to joke about. It's quite sad. She is delirious and confused and all she says is, 'I will kill him! I will kill him!' And she just repeats it all day. I would guess the strain of the job was just too much for her to take and she needs rest. Also boys, there will be no gym class until a substitute gym teacher can be found."

"What happened to the coach?" asked a student who happened to be one of the big guys.

"I don't know all the details, but I know he was experiencing pains in his chest, which fortunately they found wasn't a heart attack, but instead an anxiety attack. He has also been committed to the sanitarium for observation and treatment."

"You mean, committed to Twisted Pines?"

"No."

"Loco-Mocos?"

"No."

"The Kipper Snack Shack?"

"No."

"The insane asylum?"

"Well, yes, but it's much nicer to just say the sanitarium, or better yet, let's just call it Twin Pines Care Center. Mental health is nothing to make fun of." (She was right, but as everyone knows, some people can be very insensitive.) The substitute teacher went on. "Now, just because I'm a substitute, I don't want anyone thinking that this is going to be a party. Open your books to chapter five."

It was then that Scott managed to make it to class. "Sorry I'm late," said Scott, then he looked around. "Hey, where's Mrs. Hommophelus?"

"She had a problem and we'll leave it at that. I am your substitute."

"Oh, good. I thought I was in the wrong classroom again," said Scott.

"Take your seat and open your book to chapter five."

Scott went to his seat and sat down. The rest of the day was about the same as every other day when two of your teachers have been committed to a mental institution.

CHAPTER 21
MORE SPY STUFF

After school, the two spy buddies were at Scott's house, (that would be Scott and Jimmy-002 Mad-Dog Asparagus). This was also fairly common. What was out of the ordinary was that Stacy was there too.

"We've got to watch him closely," said Jimmy, "I'm sure he's trying to take over the world."

"Take over the world?" said Stacy, "Honestly! That is so yesterday, you two."

"He's insane and he's doing something," said Scott.

"Scott, this is the twenty-first century: no one tries to take over the world anymore. He's probably just smuggling drugs or something."

"He doesn't look like a drug smuggler. He looks crazy, like an insane scientist," said Jimmy.

"I'm really sure . . ." said Stacy.

Scott interrupted, "He does look like some kind of a crazy guy, and he was wearing a white coat."

"I think it's more like both of you are crazy," Stacy said, "and you two are supposed to be the brains of our school."

"We've got to keep an eye on him," said Jimmy.

Scott turned to Stacy, "Why don't you come with us? It's really kind of cool there. He's living in that castle that was moved one stone at a time from England. It's really beautiful, our lookout is right on a cliff—could be kind of romantic."

"No way," said Stacy. "If you guys are going to do your little romantic spy stuff, you're going to have to do it by yourself. I have homework. Maybe you two don't, but the rest of us on the planet have to study."

"Really, Stacy: it will be fun," said Scott.

"It won't be *my* idea of fun," said Stacy.

She went to the door and left.

"Wait!" called Scott. But she didn't stop.

"Let her go. This could be some dangerous stuff," said Mad Dog. "It wouldn't be safe to bring a girl along."

"Let's not take it too seriously, Jimmy. He's probably not doing anything wrong," Scott said.

"Taking over the world is definitely wrong. We may be the only ones who can stop him," said Jimmy.

"Stacy was just starting to like me again."

"Saving the world can come with a cost and it can be a little inconvenient at times," said Jimmy.

Scott just sighed. They gathered their spy stuff, plus two sandwiches and a carrot and headed towards the castle.

CHAPTER 22
THE CASTLE

On the cliff across from the castle, Jimmy and Scott sat on the green grassy edge. The sky was blue, no wind, no rain and the sun was out. All at once, a fierce storm started up immediately around the castle. Wind blew and rain and hail fell as lighting struck. Scott and Jimmy watched in amazement, since it was completely dry where they were.

The storm lasted for about three minutes, then as quickly as it started, it stopped, broke up and there was no sign of anything happening at all. The sky became blue again and the sun came out.

"Even Stacy would have to agree,

something crazy is going on inside of that castle," said Jimmy, "and whatever it is, it's making the weather go crazy around it. I'm figuring out a way of getting in there."

Jimmy stood up and loaded his spy things in his backpack.

About this time, Lambert and Barbara came out of the castle.

"Get down, Jimmy, they're there," whispered Scott loudly. Jimmy quickly got down and watched.

Lambert and Barbara got into a car and with a garage door opener lowered the drawbridge and drove away, leaving the drawbridge down.

"Now's our chance," said Jimmy, as he headed towards the castle.

"Wait. We can't go in there," called Scott.

"We have to," said Jimmy. "Who else is going to save the world?"

Scott followed Jimmy, who ran across the bridge and up to the front door. Jimmy pulled a large door handle and the door opened.

"Hey, look, it's open."

Scott was coming behind him.

"Wait," called Scott. But it was too late. Jimmy had already entered. Scott followed him into the castle.

Inside the castle, they looked around. It was decorated exactly like the old castles in England. In a long entry hall, there was a row of suits of armor, each holding a battle axe and a sword. There were also large chandeliers and ornate paintings covering the walls.

"I told you this guy is crazy," said Jimmy. "Look."

Jimmy pointed to a hand embroidered picture in a frame. The picture showed a nice little house with sunbeams in the background. There was a caption on it, which read:

"I control the weather. I'll control the world."

"You were right, Jimmy. The guy is going to try to take over the world," said Scott. "We got to be careful—he may be nuts. He could have set traps or something."

They continued to walk down the hall, using more caution than before.

As they walked, Scott stepped on a small button that was hidden in the mosaic tiles on the floor and was snatched up in a net. He hung a few feet above Jimmy.

"Scott," said Jimmy, "what did you do?"

"I didn't do anything! Get me down!"

Jimmy jumped up and grabbed the net and hung on. His weight didn't have any effect at all on the net, and Scott stayed suspended.

"See if there is a release lever or switch or something somewhere," said Scott.

"Hey!" said Jimmy excitedly, "I got my spy knife."

He reached into one front pocket, then into the other, each time pulling out nothing.

"Sorry. My mom must have washed my pants," said Jimmy.

"Find the release. There has to be one somewhere."

On a wall not too far from Scott, there were seven light switches. Jimmy went to them and flipped one. All of the suits of armor came alive. They started to chop with their battleaxes and swung their swords around. If anyone had been close, it would have been messy. After each suit of armor had swung their axes and swords six times, they stopped. The armor, axes and swords returned to their previous positions.

"Dang," said Scott.

Jimmy flipped the second switch.

With a snap, two nets were triggered and hung empty in the air.

"You're getting closer," said Scott.

Jimmy flipped the third switch.

A huge chandelier dropped to the floor. It

was so large that it would have killed or maimed ten people had they been under it.

He flipped the fourth switch.

Huge spears shot out of one wall and stuck into another. The spears shot a few inches under Scott, but only a half of an inch over Jimmy head.

Jimmy said, "Dang!"

He flipped the fifth one.

With a loud clang, a large trapdoor dropped open. The trapdoor was located in the middle of the hall and was about five feet from the front door.

Jimmy flipped the sixth.

A machine gun started to fire bullets along the wall. It started at one corner and rapidly worked its way toward Jimmy. The machine gun was breaking everything in its line of fire and leaving holes all along the wall, from the ceiling to the floor. It moved closer and closer to Jimmy and I would have to say that just when I figured Jimmy was a goner, he turned off the switch and the machine gun stopped firing.

Both Jimmy and Scott breathed a sigh of relief. There was only one switch left. Jimmy went to flip it.

"Be careful. That switch could do

anything," said Scott.

"I know, but it may let you down," said
Jimmy.

Both were nervous as he flipped the last
switch. The light in the hall turned on and that
was all.

"Isn't that just like a crazy guy?" asked
Jimmy.

Out in front of the castle a car pulled up. It
was Lambert.

"I heard a car. Oh no, they're back! We're
dead!" said Jimmy.

"You gotta hide. I'll be all right," said
Scott. "Just try to get out and get help."

"What are you going to do?" asked Jimmy.

"I'll tell him I'm the paper boy or
something. Just hide."

Both were scared as they heard the sound
of the car door opening. After a moment, they
heard the sound of it closing. Jimmy hid near
the front door, behind a coat rack with two
coats hanging on it. The rack and the coats
were full of bullet holes from the machine gun.

In walked Lambert holding two tall bags of
groceries. With the bags covering his view, he
didn't see that the trap door was open.

"Hey, Barb, we left the front door wide
open when we . . ." Lambert fell, with a scream

through the open trap door.

In walked Barbara, also carrying groceries. She stopped and screamed as she saw Scott hanging from the ceiling. She dropped her groceries which fell down through the trap door.

From below the sounds of thumps and "ouches" were heard as cans and bottles followed the same path that Lambert had taken. Barbara almost fell into the hole, herself. She teetered and teetered, but didn't fall.

"Oh no!" she cried, "I broke a nail!"

While the cans were dropping and thudding, and the "ouches" were rising from the dungeon, Jimmy slipped out the front door.

"Hi," said Scott, acting as if nothing was wrong. "My name is Scott Mitchell. I didn't mean to startle you, but I was wondering if you would like to buy a ticket to the Twin Pine High School production of *Hopping Down the Bunny Trail*? It's pretty good. I'm Peter Cottontail."

"I don't know, I'll have to ask Lambert. He makes all the big decisions like that," she said. Then she yelled down the trap door. "Hey, honey, do you want to go to a high school stage play? There is a boy here selling tickets."

There was no answer.

"Maybe it would be best if I came back at a better time," offered Scott.

"Oh, no. It's no trouble. Lambert is always falling down that stupid trap door."

Outside of the castle, Jimmy ran to where his bike waited. He took it and frantically rode down the hill. Of course, riding as frantically as he was, he was lucky not to be hit by cars, buses, low-flying airplanes and spaceships, as he raced to contact the police.

CHAPTER 23
CAPTIVATED

Back in the castle, it took about fifteen minutes for Lambert to get out of the dungeon. He didn't want to buy a ticket to the high school stage production and worse yet, he had Scott's hands and feet tied to a chair and a piece of duct tape covering his mouth. Lambert was pacing back and forth, like an excitable tiger in a cage.

"So, you thought you could disrupt my

plans, spoil my salad and wrinkle my $15 shirt that came with a tie?" asked Lambert. "Well, you're wrong. It won't happen. I'll tell you why. It is *I* who will be raining on *your* parade. It is I who will be raining on *everyone's* parade!" Lambert laughed insanely. "I control the weather. Soon...I will control the world."

Scott mumbled something which couldn't be understood because of the tape over his mouth. Lambert went to him and ripped the tape off his mouth.

"Ouch!" said Scott.

"What is it? You want to perhaps worship me now? Try to get on my good side? You seem like a likeable kid. Maybe you want to become my sidekick?" asked Lambert.

"No. I was just wondering if I couldn't get something to eat and maybe use the bathroom," said Scott.

"No! I'm the king of the whole stinking world, not some two-bit waitress. And you're just going to have to hold it until I decide what to do with you."

"I'm sorry. How about this. You just let me go. I'll get a quick burger or maybe a carrot or two, then I'll be right back. I'll even tie myself up, until you can decide what to do with me," offered Scott.

"Ah..." Lambert thought for a moment. "No. Kids don't eat carrots. What do you think I am, crazy?"

"Actually, I love carrots. And isn't being crazy a prerequisite for someone to be, when they're taking over the world?" asked Scott.

"Watch yourself, little boy. How would you like to be in the middle of a tornado? Lighting, hail, high winds and all that? It would pick your chair right up. I could do that."

Scott thought about it. "No. I don't think I would like that at all."

"Of course you wouldn't. With the lighting and all, you would really hate it. It hurts. So hold your tongue, boy, because I'm tired of fiddling with you."

"I'm sorry," Scott said trying to be quiet. "It's just that I'm pretty hungry."

"Barbara, would you get this boy something to eat before he drives me mad?"

"But we don't have much food in the house. We dropped most of it into the dungeon and once it's been in there, I'm not eating it," said Barbara. Then speaking mostly to Scott, "I think someone used to keep crocodiles in there."

"Just get what we have. I'm much too busy to mess with either of you."

"We'll, I'll look," said Barbara, "but I can't really guarantee anything."

––––––––––––

Down the hill, Jimmy found a phone booth, which was just what he wanted. He hopped off his bike, raced to the phone and dialed some numbers. "Emergency. How may I help you?" asked a voice on the other end of the phone.

"This is an emergency! I need the police!" Jimmy said, almost shouting.

"Please hold," came the reply.

While Jimmy waited for the police, pleasant elevator music played. The music was so sweet, calming and nice that it almost made Jimmy's head explode—elevator music should never be listened to when someone is in the middle of saving the world.

"Captain Penski speaking. What's the nature of your emergency?"

"This is Mad Dog Asparagus," said Jimmy. (He may have listened to the elevator music way too long.) "I mean, I'm just Mad Dog," he went on. "Some crazy guy is trying to take over the world and he's kidnapped my friend Scott while doing it."

"Mr. Asparagus, this is an emergency line,"

said Captain Penski.

"Sorry about the Mad Dog stuff, it's just my spy-code name, but this really is an emergency. The crazy guy is controlling the weather. He wants to control the world." Jimmy was much happier with how it came out that time.

"Young man, clear this emergency line at once."

The phone went dead.

Jimmy dialed the phone again.

"Police, please," said Jimmy.

"Captain Penski speaking. What is the nature of your emergency?"

"I'm not kidding! He's going to take over the world! We've got to stop him!" yelled Jimmy.

"Young man Asparagus, it's obvious that you have an active imagination. How would you like to spend your youth and your active imagination in a detention center or a reform school? Now clear this line!"

"No, wait just a minute. My friends and I just stole a bunch of candy bars from Bill's Grocery on ninth and we're going up to the old castle to eat them right now. And you can't do anything about it because you're dumb, smelly and a total geek!" said Jimmy as he hung up the phone. Jimmy got back on his bike and rode toward the castle.

CHAPTER 24
THE CAVALRY COMETH

*I*n the old westerns, when it was the darkest hour for the hero, the cavalry would ride in, which would actually make them the heroes, but nonetheless, everyone was always glad to see them because the bad guy was about to get his just desserts (which is no dessert at all).

There was a long steep road which led to the cliff and the castle across from it. Up this long road drove a single police car. In the police car sat two policemen. The first one spoke.

"Rotten kids. Stealing candy bars, then planning on eating them up at the old castle. You know, it was moved here one brick at a time from England."

"Well, don't worry. We'll catch them and when we do, it'll be the last time they steal candy bars on our patrol," said the second.

"There's the castle," said the first.

"Wow! It's kind of pretty up here. Almost romantic."

The first officer looked at the second with a half raised eyebrow.

They stopped the car fifty feet from the drawbridge, which happened to still be down. Both looked at the castle.

"Think we should drive to it, or walk?" asked the first.

"I think we should case out the place from the car until we finish our chocolate milk," said the second.

"Good idea," said the first, and both sat and drank their chocolate milk.

Now, while the cops got all chocolate milked-up, Jimmy was riding his bike back up the hill. The ride was hard and long. Poor Jimmy peddled and peddled until his legs burned and he was still only halfway to the castle. He had to stop and rest.

———————

In the castle, Scott wished he was on his

bike heading anywhere, instead of being tied up with duct tape on his mouth. Barbara walked up to Lambert, who was working frantically on his machine.

"Dear, we're completely out of food and there are two cops in a police car parked outside."

"You're kidding! What would they be doing here? We haven't done anything wrong besides deciding to take over the world," said Lambert.

"We took a hostage," pointed out Barbara.

"Way to go, kid. Get us in trouble, will you?" said Lambert. "Well, what do you got to say for yourself?" Lambert went to Scott and ripped the tape off of his mouth.

"Ow!" said Scott. "Can't we just leave the tape off and I'll be quiet?"

"I'll bet you'd like that, wouldn't you?" asked Lambert.

Scott thought for a moment, wondering if it was a trick question. "Well, yeah. It wouldn't hurt as bad as you pulling the tape off every five seconds."

"No way. If I leave the tape off, you'll probably start whistling or humming or doing something to drive me nuts, won't you?" asked Lambert.

"I'm sure it's too late for that," said Scott softly.

"What do you mean?" asked Lambert.

"Nothing."

Lambert squinted and looked at Scott very closely.

After a moment, Scott couldn't stand it. "All right, put the tape back on, but you have to promise to *leave* it on," said Scott.

"No way. I'm not putting the tape back on until you tell me how you signaled the cops," Lambert said, as he thought out loud. "What do you got, a helper? Or maybe a telephone in your shoe?" He pulled off one of Scott's shoes looked at it and smelled it. He pulled a face. "You know they have sprays that would help you with the foot odor."

"The sprays don't work," said Scott. Lambert sniffed a shoe again. "Dang, that's bad." He handed the shoes to Barbara. "Barbara, check this shoe out. I think it has a telephone in it."

"What about the cops? Shouldn't you do something?" asked Barbara.

"Oh yeah. I almost forgot. First a trickle, then a flood." He went quickly to the keyboard which connected to a large machine that was covered with levers, switches and flashing lights. Lambert punched a few keys, then engaged a lever. The large machine began to whirr, click and hum as it started to operate.

"You know, I never did get to go to the bathroom." Scott raised his voice, "so if you wouldn't talk about trickles and floods, I would greatly appreciate it!"

Lambert ignored Scott, went to the window and looked out. "Let's see how they like this," said Lambert, as Barbara joined him at the window.

Back outside at the police car, a black storm developed and rain started to fall hard. The two cops looked at each other, surprised and a little nervous.

"Did you see this storm coming?" asked the first.

"No, I didn't and I think the weather man said it was going to be clear and sunny," said the second.

"Yeah, it really came up all at once, didn't it?" said the first.

"I'll say," said the second.

Both watched the rain, which continued to fall harder and harder.

"Maybe we should get that kid with the candy bars another day," said the first.

"Yeah, he'll slip up again—then we'll bust

him," said the second.

They started the car and turned on the wipers. The rain was falling so hard that the wipers were of no use.

"Maybe we should just wait until the rain stops," said the first.

"Good idea," said the second.

Not too far from the heart of the storm, which was somewhere directly over the police car, was Jimmy. The poor boy was not only riding up a steep hill, he was riding up a steep hill in the pouring rain. He fought it and fought it. He would peddle forward, but the bike would go backward. Finally, Jimmy gave up, turned around and rode his bike back down the hill.

———————————

In the castle, Lambert had both of Scott's shoes and one of his socks cut and torn into small pieces. He was working on the second sock. Barbara was looking out the window.

"All right, he doesn't have a cell phone," said Lambert mostly to himself. "But I'll bet he has a transmitter somewhere. It's got to be in your jacket."

He grabbed Scott's jacket and, using the scissors, cut it off of him from under the ropes.

"Not my jacket!" said Scott. "I don't have a transmitter anywhere. My mom is going to kill me for the shoes; now the jacket?"

"Where's the transmitter, boy?" Lambert was getting angry. "We both know you have one, so just tell me where it is and make it easier on yourself."

"I don't own a transmitter," said Scott.

"Ah! Your watch! Who do you think you are, Dick Tracy?"

"Not my watch!"

Too late: Lambert pulled off the watch and hit it with a hammer. Pieces of it went flying.

Lambert looked through the pieces. "Nope. Not in there, either."

"Honey," Barbara said from the window, "that's probably enough water—the police car just washed down the hill.

Lambert ran to the window.

"This should teach them to mess with Lambert T. Houston the First." He laughed insanely, went to the machine and punched a few buttons. He then went back to the window and opened it. The rain slowed and then stopped all at once.

Barbara took a deep breath through her nose. "I love it just after a rain. The air is so fresh and everything is clean," she said in a dreamy-romantic way.

"I like rain too," said Lambert. "I like to step on the worms that crawl out onto the sidewalks." He looked at her and smiled and nodded as if she liked that part of rain too.

She smiled weakly at him and looked outside at the fresh, clean, just-rained-on world and sighed.

CHAPTER 25
THE OTHER CAVALRY
COMETH

*J*immy-002-Mad-Dog-Asparagus, rode to Stacy's house dripping wet. He dropped his bike on the lawn, ran up to the front door and pounded on it.

Jimmy waited for a moment that seemed like an eternity, then Stacy opened the door.

"Hello, 002," she said.

"It's Mad Dog," he said.

"Oh yeah. Sorry, Jimmy. How did you get so wet?" she asked as he stood there dripping on her front porch.

"It was raining," he answered.

"No it wasn't."

"It was too, and it was raining hard up by the castle."

"Don't be silly. The sidewalks are dry here."

Jimmy looked around. The sidewalks were dry. It made him wonder only for a moment, then he blurted out. "Scott is in trouble."

"Scott is always in trouble, but he always seems to manage to wiggle out of it somehow. That's just his nature."

"No, really! The crazy guy at the castle has him. The cops won't do anything. You gotta help!" Jimmy was sincere.

"You're just teasing, aren't you?"

"No! I need a ride up to the castle."

"I can't take you. I have to get the costumes to school. Tonight's dress rehearsal."

"Please, it's raining too hard to ride there. We gotta save Scott." Jimmy was really sincere, even though the sun was shining and the walks were dry.

"Scott is just screwing around so he won't have to go to rehearsal, or he just wants me to rescue him so he'll think he owes me a kiss."

"Stacy, he's in trouble!"

"He's going to be in more trouble if he thinks he can screw up the play!"

"Please drive me up to the castle. We'll get Scott, then you can take him to the dress rehearsal," pleaded Jimmy.

"Well, okay. But I know you two are up to something. I'll play your little game, but first you've got to help me with the costumes."

Jimmy rolled his eyes.

Back at the castle, Scott was tied up, wearing only a shirt and boxer shorts. Lambert and Barbara were close to him. There was a pile of shredded clothes, no piece bigger than half-an-inch on the table.

"What am I doing?" said Lambert. "I've seen far too many movies where the transmitter was in the buttons." He pulled a button from Scott's shirt and smashed it with a hammer. He looked through the broken pieces. "Not this one." He pulled off another button and smashed it.

"I don't have a transmitter, Mr. Einstein," said Scott.

"Well, if you don't have one now, it's for *certain* you won't when I'm done . . . for certain," said Lambert.

"What?" said Barbara.

"I'm talking to the spy kid. He knows what I meant," said Lambert, as he pulled off another button.

"All right! Stop with the buttons! You got

me. I'm an F.B.C.I.A. agent and we have been watching you for years. And that button you have there is a bomb. If you don't let me go now and turn yourself in, the whole place will blow up," said Scott, and he said it in a surprisingly convincing way.

Lambert looked at Scott, then looked closely at the button. "It's not a bomb," he said weakly.

"Oh, yes it is, and it's a powerful one! Level this castle half the ground under it," said Scott.

"I don't believe it. The castle is built on solid granite," said Lambert, a little worriedly.

"It's a powerful bomb," said Scott. "It'll level the place."
"I still don't believe it," replied Lambert.
"Well, you had better," said Scott.

Lambert set the button carefully onto the counter and looked at Scott. He slowly picked up a hammer.

"No, Lambert! Don't do it! It really could be a bomb," said Barbara.

Lambert didn't take his eyes off of Scott. Scott kept a straight face. Lambert looked harder at Scott. Scott not only kept his straight face but looked harder back at Lambert and furrowed his eyebrows, all this without blinking.

Now, Lambert was really thinking about the bomb and Scott seemed completely serious in his furrowed non-blinking eyes.

Lambert started to put his hammer down, then all at once he yelled, "Ha!" He quickly raised the hammer and brought it smashing down onto the button.

"You're very lucky. It must have been a dud," said Scott.

"What are you thinking? You could have blown us all to smithereens," said Barbara.

"Of course I couldn't have. He was bluffing. This kid's only carrying transmitters—not bombs."

Back at Stacy's house, Jimmy carried a large armload of clothes out to the car. Stacy took them from him, one costume at a time and gently loaded them into her nearly full car. Jimmy's head was ready to explode as he impatiently waited while Stacy carefully avoided wrinkles.

When the last costume was finally placed into the car, Jimmy spoke. "Can we save Scott now?"

"I guess, if you have your little heart really

set on it," said Stacy.

"About time!" Jimmy went to get into the car.

"Not so fast, buddy. You're all sopping wet," said Stacy. "I have some plastic and a towel to spread out on the seat."

Jimmy thought his head was really-really-really ready to explode, but it didn't as he waited and waited for Stacy to neatly spread out plastic and a towel on the seat of her car for him.

Meanwhile, back at the castle, Scott was still tied up, wearing only underwear and a piece of tape on his mouth. Lambert and Barbara stood by the door.

"We're going to get food," said Lambert. "Not so much for you; we'll need it anyway when we take over the world."

With the tape on his mouth, Scott wasn't expected to answer. Lambert continued, "I don't want you messing around with anything while I'm gone." Lambert left the room, then he popped his head back in.

"And I mean it! Don't touch nothin'!"

Lambert left again and Scott rolled his eyes.

The cavalry (Jimmy and Stacy) were heading up the hill toward the castle.

"Okay, that's the castle," said Jimmy.

"I can't believe how mad I am at Scott right now," said Stacy. "You guys were going to play spies around this castle until you got in trouble and got me involved."

Just about then, Lambert drove his car across the drawbridge and onto the road.

"Oh, no! That's the crazy guy's car," said Jimmy as he ducked down.

"What do you want me to do?" panicked Stacy.

"Just keep driving up the hill," said Jimmy. "Try to act normal."

(But I'll tell you, she was too nervous to act normal. She pulled a kind of silly face and tried to smile as she continued to drive.)

In Lambert's car, Lambert saw a pretty girl with deep wading pool blue eyes and a silly grin on her face drive by.

"Hey, you know that girl?" asked Lambert.

"No. I don't think so," said Barbara

"Does she seem to be acting funny to you?" asked Lambert.

"Well, yeah, but all girls at that age act funny," said Barbara.

"Yeah. Probably driving around looking for boys," said Lambert, thinking he had the whole world figured out.

Back in Stacy's car, Jimmy was hiding on the floor. Stacy was driving, trying to act normal.

"They're gone, but I think they were watching me. The guy does look crazy," said Stacy.

"I told you he was. Just keep driving. I'll watch to see if they're following us," said 002 as he got up from the floor and looked out the back window.

"Okay, but I'm really scared now," said Stacy.

"It's fine. They're not following us. Just pull to the side of the road and park," said Jimmy.

Stacy parked the car a short distance up the hill from the castle.

"Okay, come on. I may need your help," said Jimmy.

"I'm not going snooping around in anyone's house—especially some crazy guy's castle!" said Stacy.

"I have to save Scott!" Jimmy got out of the car and ran toward the castle.

"Hurry, the crazy guy could come back," said Stacy, but she didn't really have to, as Jimmy was running at full speed.

Stacy stayed in the car for a moment, then

she shook her head. She slowly got out of the car and walked down the hill. Jimmy was way ahead of her. She began to jog first, then started to run after him.

"Wait up," she called. "I don't want to be left out here alone!"

Jimmy didn't even slow down a little.

In the castle, Scott was still tied up, wearing only boxer shorts and duct tape on his mouth. (The tape was on his mouth—the boxer shorts were where boxer shorts should be.) He struggled to get free. A green glow appeared in his eyes and the heavy ropes stretched but didn't break. The green glow grew brighter as Scott struggled some more. Suddenly there was the sound of a door opening.

Scott quit trying to escape and the green glow disappeared.

Stacy entered the room. She was nervous.

"Oh no, Scott! You're nearly naked!" She covered her eyes the best she could. "002 just got caught in a net. You want me to untie you?"

She took the tape off of Scott's mouth.

"Yes, please. Jimmy was right. The guy's

crazy. He's found a way to control the weather and he's going to try to take over the world, now," said Scott.

"Is he a pervert, too?" asked Stacy.

"No, he just thought I had a transmitter hidden on me."

"Where are your clothes?"

With his hands tied, Scott nodded at the pile of ripped and shredded clothes and pointed to it with his lips.

"There," he said.

Stacy untied the ropes. Scott stood up. Stacy covered her eyes.

"Well, hurry and put them on. You're embarrassing me."

"He shredded my clothes."

"Oh. We've got to get out of here. I'll try to get 002 free."

"First I have to figure out how to stop this machine," said Scott.

Stacy left the room. Scott went to the machine and looked to see what he could do to it. He looked it over with a slight green glow in his eyes, then took a frying pan and hit the side of the machine with it.

It wasn't much of a hit and it looked as if nothing would happen. Scott was ready to hit it again when sparks started to fly and a flame shot out.

Scott jumped back as a rain cloud formed and huge drops of rain started to fall in the room. The storm quickly grew bigger and more violent. Lighting struck and exploded a hanging light fixture.

Scott got a worried look on his face and ran out of the room as lighting struck the door, then the wall and then the light fixture again.

In the front hall of the castle, Jimmy was lying on the floor tangled in a net. Stacy was trying to help untangle him, but she wasn't doing very well.

Scott ran into the hall.

"Boy, Scott! Am I ever glad to see you!" said Jimmy.

"Me too. We've got to get out of here quickly. I think I might have messed with the weather making machine too much," said Scott.

Scott grabbed Jimmy, net and all, picked him up and ran out the door.

"What did you do, Scott?" called Stacy.

She looked back toward the room where the machine was. Her eyes got big as she saw a river of water flooding toward her. She ran out the front door and slammed it behind her.

Outside the castle, Scott, still wearing only

his underwear, carried Jimmy in the net. Stacy was close behind.

"Stacy's car is right up the hill," called Jimmy. "Hey, where's your clothes?"

"The crazy guy shredded them all," he said.

Scott ran up the hill to the car. He opened the door and tossed Jimmy into the back seat, net and all. He climbed into the front seat as Stacy got into the driver's seat.

"Here Scott, wear this," said Stacy, as she reached back and grabbed a costume.

"Now maybe the cops will believe us," said Jimmy.

"Of course they will," said Scott as he put on the costume.

"Stacy, we've got to get to the police, fast!" said Jimmy.

"I have to get the costumes to the rehearsal," said Stacy. "What am I thinking? That will wait. We've got to report that crazy guy."

Scott finished putting on the costume. He was very wet and cold. "They'll take us seriously, now." Scott said as he pulled on the hood. The costume was his rabbit suit—large puffy ears, big floppy feet, fluffy tail and all.

CHAPTER 26
THE POLICE REPORT

Everything was normal in the police station when Scott walked in, wearing his rabbit costume. He was accompanied by Stacy and Jimmy. They approached the front desk. "We need to report a man who is planning to take over the world," said Scott to a sergeant.

Across the station, Captain Penski looked up from his desk. He shook his head in disgust as he got up and walked toward the front desk.

"There's a crazy guy living in the old castle who is trying to take over the world. He's found a way to control the weather and he's . . ."

Captain Penski came up to the desk. "If these kids are telling you anything about stealing candy bars or someone taking over the world, arrest them for obstruction of justice and interfering with the due process of law."

"We're serious! We got proof! He really *is* crazy and he can control the weather," said Scott.

Penski looked at Scott in the rabbit suit.

"In my precinct, a large rabbit has no right to call anyone else crazy," said Penski. "I want you and your little bunny friends out of here now!"

Stacy was shocked by the captain's rudeness.

"Scott is telling the truth! The crazy guy had him tied up. He can control the weather. It was raining inside his house so hard that it was starting to flood."

"If you kids don't get out of here in eight seconds, I'm going to arrest you all. In fact, I'm tempted to test you for drugs and hold you for the night and have your parents pick you up tomorrow. Now beat it, or else."

Stacy wanted to explode all over the captain. Scott took her arm.

"Let's go, Stacy," said Scott. "We're sorry you feel we're bothering you again, but we are telling the truth."

They left the station.

Outside the police station, Stacy let it out: "I can't believe it! He thinks we're lying or on drugs."

"I'll bet he'll feel dumb when the world gets taken over from his jurisdiction," Jimmy said.

Stacy looked at her watch. "Oh no! Scott, we've got to get to rehearsal. Come on, 002; we'll give you a ride."

"It's Mad Dog."

"Sorry, I forgot. Mad Dog."

They all got into the car and drove away.

CHAPTER 27
THE WORLD'S SHORTEST BUT MOST EXCITING CHAPTER WITH THE LONGEST TITLE

At the castle, both Lambert and Barbara got out of their car and walked toward the front door. Each carried sacks of groceries.

"I hope that kid appreciates this," said Lambert. "I don't even *like* carrots."

"I'm sure he'll appreciate it. I think it was very nice of you," said Barbara.

At the front door, neither Lambert nor Barbara noticed the water leaking all around the frame. Lambert barely touched the doorknob when the door burst open and a whole flood of water came out.

Luckily for Barbara, she was standing off to one side of the main flow of water. The flood caught Lambert, washing him down the walk and over the side of the drawbridge. Lambert grabbed and clung to the side of the drawbridge. The water slowed, then stopped.

"I'll get that kid!" yelled Lambert.

"Oh no, oh no! My shoes!" yelled Barbara. "These are Italian and they're not supposed to get wet!"

(Exciting wasn't it? The door burst open and water came out. Dang exciting . . . . Oh, never mind.)

CHAPTER 28
DRESS REHEARSAL

*S*cott and Stacy entered the back of the school's auditorium, carrying all the costumes except the large rabbit suit...Scott was still wearing that.

Mr. Phillips saw them. "We'll, it's about

time! I'll tell you one thing: dress rehearsal is especially slow when no one is dressed."

"You wouldn't believe the excuse that we have," said Stacy, "so I'm not even going to try to tell you."

"She's right," said Scott.

"Well, Scott," said Mr. Phillips, "I am glad to see that you are ready."

They walked up to him, dropped the costumes they were holding, then walked backstage.

"All right, Stars!" called Mr. Phillips. "Let's get dressed."

The actors went and took their costumes from the two piles.

"And please hurry. Our rehearsal time is cut about as short as it can be," continued Mr. Phillips.

While the actors were getting dressed, Stacy and Scott moved away from the others.

"Scott, what are we going to do?" asked Stacy.

"I think his machine is broken enough that we'll be okay for a while, but we've got to find someone to believe us," said Scott.

"I'm scared," said Stacy.

"Don't worry, I won't let anything happen to you." He hugged her.

"Come on, Peter," called Mr. Phillips. "Let's get this show on the road."

Scott walked toward center stage then turned back to Stacy.

"It's okay. We'll be all right. I promise."

Backstage, a stage hand was watching a small black and white TV. On it, a newscaster was reading from a sheet in front of her. "In other news, Twin Pine City has been experiencing some of the strangest weather patterns ever, with over five feet of rain falling in some areas of the city in the last twenty-four hours. Other areas of the city are completely dry." The stage hand changed the channel.

After the dress rehearsal, Scott and Stacy were talking in the parking lot next to Stacy's car. "Don't worry," said Scott. "If he messes with you or me, I'll just have to hit his weather machine with a frying pan again."

"That is so crazy that that did anything," said Stacy. "A frying pan?"

"That's all I had."

Mr. Phillips walked by, noticed them and spoke. "Scott, I know you've been getting into your character lately, and I love it—but I really would rather you didn't wear your costume home at night."

"It's a long story, Mr. Phillips, but this is all I have to wear tonight," said Scott.

"Oh? How strange. I'll see you both here tomorrow. Big opening night!" Mr. Phillips said, sounding very excited and a little nervous.

Mr. Phillips went towards his car.

"You know, he's probably going to try to come after you," said Stacy.

"What are the chances of having the starring role in the play and having to save the whole world, both in the same week?" asked Scott.

"Come on Scott. Let me give you a ride home."

"I think it would be best if I walked. After saving me from Lambert T. Houston, you're just looking too good for me to behave myself."

"Is that right?"

"Oh yes. But I also need to work on my lines and figure out some way to save the world. I can't leave it all up to Jimmy."

"It's Mad Dog," said Stacy.

"That's right," said Scott.

They looked at each other, he into her

wading pool blue eyes, she into his golf course green eyes.

"I was thinking we...I mean, it may be OK if we kissed a little" said Stacy. She kissed Scott.

"Wow! I'm more than tempted. I mean, like, totally, but I'm wearing a rabbit suit and I really need to sort my thoughts. Are we having any tests tomorrow?" he asked.

"It wouldn't matter; you'd ace them anyway." she said

"I don't know, maybe," said Scott. "I've kind of been lucky lately. I'll see you tomorrow." He walked away, then turned back to her. "Hey, if you wouldn't mind picking me up for school tomorrow, I would let you."

"I wouldn't mind at all."

"Then I'll see ya tomorrow." He turned and walked away.

Stacy watched him for a moment. He stopped and turned back again.

"Hey, if the play goes well, and no one takes over the world tomorrow night . . . you think maybe I could have four kisses?" asked Scott. "One for the play, one for the world not getting taken over and one for you saving me today."

"That's only three. What's the forth one

for?" said Stacy with a smile.

"That would be just for fun," said Scott.

"Yeah, I would like that."

"Then, I'll see you tomorrow."

Scott continued to walk. Stacy got into her car and drove away.

Scott walked the dark streets of Twin Pines with many thoughts and worries on his mind. He worried about his lines, and about the fate of the world, and how he was going to tell his mom about his shoes and jacket without making her worry too much.

As Scott walked, the gang of bullies he encountered before saw him. One of the bullies yelled, "Hey, look guys, we're in luck! It's the Easter Bunny."

"I think we should rattle him and see if we can't shake out some candy," said the big one. "What do you think, boys?"

"Yeah! Let's take the Easter Bunny's candy," said the one with the higher pitched voice.

Scott, still not noticing them, turned just enough that they saw his face for the first time since the last time they met.

"Hey, it's the kid that kicked all of our

butts!" said one.

"He didn't kick my *butt*—he kicked my head, like seven times!" said another.

"I'm getting out of here before he does it again," said another.

"Me too," said another.

The whole gang ran away feeling that the streets weren't as safe for them as they once thought they were. Scott didn't even notice them as they scampered off. Scott also didn't notice a white van that pulled up next to him. He didn't notice the side door of the white van opening, nor the net gun aimed and fired at him. Scott did, however, notice the net that had covered him. He also noticed being dragged into the white panel van and being driven away. It was then, tangled in a net— inside the van that Scott started thinking about how much more he would've rather been kissing Stacy and forgetting about all the other important thoughts that he thought were so important to be thinking about just a moment before.

CHAPTER 29
THE RABBIT RAISINS HIT THE FAN

*T*he next morning was a lovely morning (as far as mornings go) when Stacy pulled into Scott's driveway and honked the horn twice.

She waited a moment, then honked again. She rolled down the window and yelled, "Scott, are you coming or not?"

She noticed for the first time that clouds were building around the area. Jimmy came running, stopped at the passenger car door and looked in the window.

"Hi, Stacy. Where's Scott?"

"Late as usual," said Stacy. "How are you doing, Mad Dog?"

"Hey, you got my name right—that's one time in a row," said Jimmy excitedly.

"Yeah, it's kind of a record," said Stacy.

"So what's keeping Scott?" asked Jimmy.

"I don't know. I was supposed to give him a ride to school today."

"Maybe the crazy guy got him," said Jimmy.

"Jimmy," she said skeptically, "he had a lot on his mind—he probably forgot and already went to school. I may as well take you. Hop in. It looks like it's going to rain."

Jimmy got into the car.

Stacy backed the car out of the driveway and headed down the street. Outside of the car, it rain harder and harder.

"Have you ever seen rain like this before?" asked Stacy.

"Just the once when I was trying to ride my bike to the crazy guy's castle," answered Jimmy.

"Really? Was it raining hard then? Because I thought you were just making it up, maybe squirted yourself with a hose."

"No, it was raining just like this."

An announcement came over the radio. "Flash flood warnings are posted throughout the state as heavy rainfall is occurring over the region. A Travelers' Advisory is in effect."

Stacy pulled the car to the side of the road.

They watched the rain fall so hard that they couldn't see out of the car's windows.

Stacy and Jimmy looked at each other, then both spoke at once and said the same thing; "He has Scott!"

Inside Lambert's castle, Scott was tied up in the chair wearing his rabbit costume with his mouth taped. Lambert was working with his machine while Barbara sat close by eating a carrot.

"The world will now fall under my power. And there's nothing you can do, you screwy rabbit," said Lambert, then he laughed like Elmer Fudd. (If you don't know who Elmer Fudd is, it may be time to look up one of the old Bugs Bunny cartoons.) Lambert thought for a moment and then continued. "I don't know what you did to my machine yesterday, but I'm going to give you a chance to explain."

He pulled off the tape from over Scott's mouth.

"Would you cut it out with the tape already?" said Scott, rather annoyed.

"Tell me, Mr. Rabbit," said Lambert, "how did you program the machine to rain in the house?"

"Well, I . . . I . . . I just . . . just . . ."

Lambert didn't let him finish. "Don't you try stalling with me. Taking over the world doesn't leave me that much extra time to monkey around."

"I wasn't stalling, I was just trying to think of exactly what I did," said Scott.

"Well, it doesn't matter what you did, I was able to fix it. It wasn't easy, mind you," he said, raising his voice, "because everything was wet and I nearly electrocuted myself to death about seven times! But I fixed it, anyway."

"Yeah and today he's going to take over the world," said Barbara. "He said so, himself."

"It is going to rain so hard and so long that you and the rest of the world will be wishing you had an ark."

"Oh, you don't want to do that," said Scott.

"I do, too! This whole world will be mine. Under one government: the United Government of Me, Lambert T. Houston the

First," said Lambert.

"And I get to be the Vice-King of the whole world," said Barbara.

"Don't take over the world today," said Scott.

"And why not—or are you pulling one of those 'please Lambert, don't throw me in the briar patch?'" asked Lambert.

"No, I wouldn't do that; I'm Peter in the Twin Pine High School production of *The Bunny Trail.* Opening night is tonight. If you take over the world today, there will be a lot of disappointed kids who bought their tickets in advance."

"Boy, I guess there would be," said Barbara in a very concerned manner.

"Don't listen to him. He's just grabbing for anything," said Lambert.

"No, really! I'm the star; I can even hook you up with some free tickets if you don't take over the world today," said Scott.

Lambert put the tape back over Scott's mouth.

"The kids are going to have to learn that disappointment is a part of life. I don't have any time for plays; I'm taking over the world and I'm taking over the world now," said Lambert.

Barbara looked concerned as Lambert went back to his machine.

"You mean, we're not going to be able to go to any plays after we take over the world?" asked Barbara.

"We'll go to a hundred plays. Now be quiet and let me work."

He started typing some more on the keyboard. Barbara went to him. "What are you doing now?"

"Just turned the rain on in the southern hemisphere," said Lambert.

"Oh, really?" asked Barbara.

"And if you're quiet, I'll get it raining in Europe and the rest of the world by noon."

He continued to type on the keyboard.

"Well then, I'd better be quiet." She continued to eat her carrot.

———————

At the police station, it was raining as hard as it was raining in many areas of the world.

Stacy and Jimmy pulled up and ran into the station. They went to the front desk. All the officers were looking out the window.

Jimmy reached up and rang the bell (perhaps that would be rung the bell—I've been advised that in some part of the universe that would be rang the dang bell, rung the bell, but never rung the dung bell—I'm sorry, I humor myself again.) We'll go with rang, which is correct. Jimmy rang the bell.

Captain Penski looked at them, and not being much of a rainy-day person anyway, he went to the front desk. "First thing that I want to say kids is relax: no one tries to take over the world when it's raining like this."

"He's going to take over the world *with* rain like this!" said Jimmy.

"Where is your rabbit friend, Mr. Asparagus?" asked Captain Penski.

"I'm Jimmy; his name is Scott—the crazy guy has kidnapped him again!" said Jimmy.

"Is that right? Follow me. We need to talk privately," said Penski, nodding to the officers looking out the window. "Some of them may be in on it."

"It's about time you decided to listen," said Jimmy.

"I just hope it's not too late." said Stacy.

Penski, led Stacy and Jimmy into a holding cell.

"What are we doing in here?" asked Jimmy.

Once Stacy and Jimmy were inside, Captain Penski left the cell and slammed the door.

"When the rain stops," Penski said, "I'll be calling your parents to pick you up."

"The rain isn't going to stop, Sergeant Poop-for-Brains! It's going to keep falling until there is nothing that anyone can do!" yelled Jimmy. "That crazy guy is going to take over the world and it's going to be all your fault!"

"That's Captain, to you," Penski said "and I'm putting the little 'Poop-for-Brains' comment on your permanent record."

"Ahhh," screamed Jimmy.

Penski left the holding cell area and slammed the door behind him.

"What are we going to do?" asked Stacy.

"The first thing that I'm going to do is tell the mayor or the governor or whoever his boss is, after the crazy guy takes over the world, and make sure he gets fired!"

Jimmy folded his arms and sat on the bench.

CHAPTER 30
OH ME, OH MY

With the rain falling like it was, the newscasters didn't have a lot of anything else to talk about. Pictures of storms and floods were on the news, as the newscasters announced the happenings. "In world news, the rain that has been hitting us has been also hitting the rest of the world. Forecasters see no sign of the rain stopping. In every major city in the world there have been reports of flooding and damage due to the sudden rainfall.

In the castle, Lambert turned the television off. Scott was still tied up, still wearing his rabbit suit and still had tape over his mouth.

Rain continued to fall outside without any sign of stopping. Lambert and Barbara watched intently out the window.

"It won't be long before I own the whole world," said Lambert.

Scott struggled with the ropes, but it was useless.

At the police station, the rain was falling hard outside, all the police were still looking out the windows as the water rose in the streets.

"I've never seen rain like this," said one of the flatfoots. (Flatfoot: a police term used for the cops who walk a beat. Beat: a term for the area in which a said flatfoot walks.)

"It's like something evil is controlling it," said another.

"yeah, totally," said another.

"The kids were telling the truth," said Penski to himself. He walked to the holding cells and unlocked the door to the cell.

"It's about time!" said Jimmy.

"I'm sorry that I didn't believe your story, but I'm believing it now," said Penski. "What can we do?" said Jimmy as he hurried out of the cell. Stacy and Penski followed close behind him.

"We have to hurry! Scott's in trouble!"

They left the holding cell.

It wasn't long before a string of wet police cars worked their way up the road in front of Lambert's castle. Each car had their lights on flashing.

In the castle, Lambert and Barbara were looking out the window as they saw the police cars. Scott was still tied up wearing the rabbit suit with duct tape covering his mouth.

"Oh no. It's the cops," said Barbara.

"I was wondering how long it would take them to get here," said Lambert. "This is going to be fun""

He went to the machine and punched buttons and pulled levers, chuckling as he did

"Watch this," Lambert said to Barbara..

Outside, the stream of cop cars drove up the hill as a darker, blacker storm gathered over the street. Suddenly, lighting struck one car, then another. The rain continued to fall harder and harder. In a short time, all the cars had washed down the hill. Lambert and Barbara continued to look out the window as they watched the cop cars all wash away.

"Ha, ha," laughed Lambert. "Never mess with Lambert T. Houston."

"Oh dear; you're so smart," gushed Barbara.

Lambert went to Scott and ripped the tape from his mouth. "Did you hear that, Rabbitman? I just washed all the cop cars away." He paused a moment, then shouted with excitement, "Washed them all down the hill!"

"You know, bad guys never get away with this kind of stuff. They always do something wrong or something stupid," said Scott.

"Other bad guys do something wrong or something stupid. Not me. The whole world will bow to me, the king of the whole planet Earth. Who knows? Maybe I'll move up from there and conquer the Universe!"

"Wow, could I be Vice-King of the whole Universe?" asked Barbara.

"Why not?" said Lambert, then he turned to Scott. "And Rabbitman, you can say that you witnessed it all first-hand. Perhaps the little bunny wants a carrot." He dangled a carrot in front of Scott's face. Scott's nose started to twitch and a green glow appeared in his eyes.

Lambert saw the green glow, got a little

nervous and pulled the carrot back quickly.

"Oh, dear! What did you do to him?" asked Barbara as she saw the green glow in Scott's eyes.

"I didn't do nothing! I just offered him a carrot," said Lambert with a look of fear on his face.

"You know you should never tease a rabbit with a carrot unless you plan on giving it to him," said Barbara.

Scott's eyes got very green and he broke the ropes that were wrapped around him.

"And that was your mistake!" shouted Scott.

Scott jumped around the room wildly—moving like a rabbit running on high-octane gasoline. He seemed to be going in all directions at once and all the time he was kicking, biting and pulling noses. At one point he double kicked Lambert in the cranium, (we discussed that...the Brainium Cranium) which knocked him to the floor. Scott then ran out of the room. The next second he returned carrying a net that he had taken from one of the traps in the entryway. With super-rabbit speed, he caught and tied up Lambert and Barbara in it.

"Nothing you can do will stop it! The

machine is set on auto. It can't be canceled without the secret code and only I know it and there is no way that I will ever tell anyone!" yelled Lambert. "You've just doomed the world."

Scott picked up the frying pan.

"Yep: the code is secret and I'll never tell! Never, never, never," ranted Lambert. "You can't stop the machine by breaking it, either; it has already started. It's in motion. Nothing can stop it. Break the machine and you'll be kissing the planet goodbye."

Scott hit the pan on the side of the machine in the same place as he hit it the first time. He stood back.

"That won't do anything. Destroy the machine and you'll destroy the world. The machine is the only way to stop the rain. It can't be stopped without the machine and the machine can't be stopped without the code and I'll never say what the code is until I own the whole world," gloated Lambert.

The machine started to spark then a little flame shot out, followed by a few more sparks. Scott looked outside and saw that the rain was stopping and the sun was coming out. The police cars were again driving up the hill. Inside, however, a huge cloud developed in the room and it began to rain. Scott grabbed an umbrella.

"Hey, that shouldn't do that!" said Lambert. "Oh, no! It's going to flood in here again. The code word is 'Trebmal' it's 'Lambert' spelled backwards. Please turn it off! Trebmal! We'll drown! Please: Trebmal! Trebmal!

Scott took a carrot. "Maybe I'll turn it off, maybe I won't, but first I want to hear both of you say that you'll never try to take over the world again," Scott said with an ever so slight grin on his face.

Water was quickly filling the room.

Lambert and Barbara both called out, "We promise that we will never try to take over the world again! Now turn it off!"

"You've got to say it five thousand times," said Scott.

"We promise that we will never try to take over the world again. We promise that we will never try to take over the world again. We promise that we will never try to take over the world again."

They went on and on and on, which is exactly what someone would have to do to say something five thousand times. From the front of the castle, there was the sound of someone pounding at the door. Then there was the sound of the front door being broken down. Then there was the sound of Penski yelling, "Police! Come on, men; let's get 'em!" Then there was the sound of Jimmy yelling, "Don't step on the . . ." Then there was the sound of the three nets being snatched up and a trapdoor falling open.

Shortly after that, Jimmy and Stacy came into the lab...and of course, it was still raining.

"Got eight cops in the nets and five went down the trapdoor," said Jimmy.

"Maybe we should help them," asked Scott.

"Oh, don't worry; there are plenty more where they came from," said Jimmy. "They brought the whole force."

Five cops entered the lab.

"In the net you'll find Lambert T. Houston, The First. The King of the Whole World and his Vice-King, Barbara."

Lambert and Barbara stopped repeating their lines. Lambert rather humbly said, "Howdy," to the police officers.

"It's a pleasure to meet you," said Barbara.

"Hey, don't stop. That's only twenty times," Scott said.

Lambert and Barbara quickly started to

repeat their line. "We promise that we will never try to take over the world again. We promise that we will…" (etc…etc…etc…).

Scott addressed one of the officers. "When they've said that four thousand nine hundred and eighty more times, punch "Lambert" spelled backwards into the machine. It's the secret code that should shut off the water."

"Thank you, son. You did mighty good work. We're all very thankful to you," said the officer.

"Oh, Scott. You saved the whole world." said Stacy.

"No. It was mostly Mad Dog," said Scott.

Scott and Jimmy did their spy handshake and both said together, "Spy-buddies, forever!"

Scott, Stacy and Jimmy left the lab while the police continued counting the number of times Lambert and Barbara said that they wouldn't try to take over the world.

In the entryway, Scott found eight police officers suspended by nets in the ceiling. Among those dangling officers, Scott saw Captain Penski.

"Kids, you saved the world," said Captain Penski, much nicer and more humble than he had ever been in the past. "If you'll get me down, I'd like to be the first to shake your hands."

"The offer is tempting," said Jimmy. "But I guess we're just going to have to settle for the Presidential Medal of Honor, instead."

"Oh come on! Let me down!" pleaded Penski.

"Not until you say, 'From now on I will not put kids in jail and act like a jerk when they tell me that someone is taking over the world,'" said Jimmy.

"All right," said Penski. "From now on I will not put kids in jail and act like a jerk when they tell me that someone is taking over the world," repeated Penski. "Now let me down."

"Not until you say it five thousand times!" said Stacy and Jimmy in unison.

The three spy friends left the castle.

CHAPTER 31
THE BUNNY TRAIL

*T*he news of Scott's heroics had spread in Twin Pines like jam on toast. That night in the high school, the halls were empty but the auditorium was full of students and proud parents as the play was in full production. Scott was on stage, wearing his now-famous bunny suit. Stacy was also wearing a bunny suit, with an apron that brought out the blue in her wading pool eyes.

"Well, well, Little Miss Bunnytune, I must say that you is the prettiest rabbit that there ever was," said Scott as he looked deep into those eyes.

"I'll bet you say that to all the bunnies you meet," said Stacy.

"I do, but this time I really means it and I really do. I really do." And Scott really did mean it too.

"Well, that's the kindest thing that I everest did hear," said Stacy. She lightly bit her bottom lip and shyly smiled to Scott.

Those two actors were in the moment and watching the moment from backstage was Mr. Phillips, who was prouder than a hen that laid a dozen eggs, all with two yokes. Standing next to Mr. Phillips was Mrs. Hommophelus, the math teacher. I'm not completely sure, but I'm pretty sure she was looking directly at Scott and was saying to herself, "I will kill him. I will kill him." And I'll be darned if standing right next to her wasn't the football coach and he was muttering something which sounded an awful lot like, "Play football. I'll make you a star. You'll be rich; I'll be rich; we'll both be rich and famous." (I'm not a hundred percent sure, but I have heard from many reliable sources that both the coach and the math teacher escaped from the funny farm together.)

Back on stage, Scott held Stacy's hand. "I'm the happiest rabbit that there ever was and has been and I think it's all because of you," Scott said as he tenderly pulled Stacy close and kissed her.

The audience stood and clapped wildly as the stars of the play kissed. A few people whistled and someone yelled (I believe it was one of the big guys from the football game who was trying to be little and geekie, or it may have just been Jimmy), "Way to go, Scott!"

The curtains closed, then opened again to find Scott and Stacy still kissing, so the curtains closed again. The audience applauded wildly.

The curtains opened again. This time, they quit kissing and started to take their bows. Mr. Phillips applauded wildly and wiped a tear from his eye.

The standing ovation lasted ten minutes. Then the audience took a break, got drinks, went to the restroom, etc., then continued the ovation for five minutes more.

CHAPTER 32
CAPTAIN'S LOG

*N*ear the pile of rabbit droppings in Scott's yard, a voice was heard which, if not properly translated, would sound like a very high pitched whoopee cushion.

"Full thrusters!" called the Captain.

"Yo-Yo, Captain." (Frenchie went with "yo-yo," because "oui, oui" was too confusing and "aye, aye," was way overused...mostly by pirates.)

The sound of the tiny little thrusters being

fired was also heard. Dust blew from the hole as the ship started to rise. It was covered with dirt and very large rabbit droppings.

It rose up and up and all looked well with it as it headed towards space. On board, all the aliens sat at their stations. The captain looked very much in control.

"Captain, we've broken away from the gravitational force of the blue planet," said the first mate.

"Set a course for the Andrewsii Galaxy," called the captain. "We have a war to fight."

Buttons were pushed and thrusters were fired.

The captain spoke again, this time into a small hand-held recorder. "Captain's log, star-date 14b2310. The crew of the BS Entrepreneur, after experiencing difficulties brought on by the Megatron Light Flinger, was forced to crash-land on a blue planet in the QZX43212987 region. We have found the blue planet to be perhaps the most unpleasant and undesirable planet in the universe. Not only is it very smelly, being made up almost entirely of doo-doo, but it rained most of the time. We would encourage all space travelers to avoid this planet in the future. I know we will."

The little ship changed direction, then blasted into deep space at an incredible speed. Only a faint, glowing vapor trail and a few rabbit raisins were left to show where the ship had been.

EPILOGUE

*T*hus, the story of Rabbitman comes to an end—and you now know the reason why, when the world is in turmoil and evil runs rampant, the city commissioner lights the bunny alert spotlight in the sky. So some night when the moon is full and you notice a lanky boy with golf course green eyes in a rabbit suit on your roof, sniffing the air for trouble, you can go back to bed knowing the world is safe with Rabbitman on the job.

Well, the world is safe until 9:00 PM—He has a curfew. He's only 14 years old.

AND NOW FOR THEN END OF THE "TAIL"

As its author, I would like to thank you for reading Rabbitman. I hope that you not only found it rewarding and fun, but, that it gave you a reason to smile. In that spirit I would like to share with you another one of my works:

Pirates, Ghosts, Zombies
and other things that make me smile

It's a refreshing collection of short stories that are really fun and intended for nearly everyone in the family. As the title suggests, there are a few stories that may be a pinch too scary for the very young, who wouldn't understand the humor of them—but overall, people of all ages love these stories. Allow me to share one from this collection with you.

THE OCEAN BLOOM

I met an old seaman who asked if I could spare some change for a meal. I'm not one to give cash away without being sure where it will be spent. So I told him that I would buy him a meal if in return he would tell me a story. He said that that would be a fine deal. We walked together to a nearby diner. I held the door and we both entered.

We found an empty booth and there took up residence. "Arrr, 'tis mighty kind of you, boy, to help out a nearly-starved, down-on-his-luck sailor," he said.

I was much too old to be called "boy," but considering his age (which I guessed must be more than eighty), I decided not to take offense.

"Feel free to order what you will and eat as much as you can," I said.

"Oh, that be very kind of ya."

"But remember: you must tell me a story. If the story is good, there will be a bonus. You will be rewarded with the dessert of your choice."

He wore a heavy rain jacket and matching hat, which were well-worn and soiled. His leather like skin was more than wrinkled; it was grooved with age and experience.

"Arrr, a story you wants? A story I can afford. My name is Robert Timpson. I first hailed from Penzance, England, but I now calls the world me home. You see, I joined the crew of a freight ship when I were but a wee minnow—a lad of only twelve—and have not been home since. I have worked on many a vessel. Served in the navies of three different countries and have fought more scurvy battles and wars than ten men should have to. I owned a ship. A beauty she were; the *Ocean Bloom*. A magnificent ship, with . . ."

The waitress interrupted us. The old seaman ordered the filet of shark with a bowl of chowder.

"Tell me, Mr. Timpson, where is the *Ocean Bloom* now?"

"You're a friend. You call me Bob Timpson . . . Captain Bob Timpson."

"Okay, Captain Bob Timpson. What happened to your ship?"

"I would tell ya, but there wouldn't be much use, since you wouldn't believe me anyway."

"Is the story of the *Ocean Bloom* true?"

"It's as true and as real as the metal plate in

me head and the harpoon point in me backside."

"You have a metal plate in your head?"

"And a harpoon point stuck in me backside—I could show you the scar, too, if ya be calling me a liar."

He stood up and began to unbuckle his pants. Diners stared and gasped. A waitress dropped her tray.

"No, no, that won't be necessary, Captain Bob Timpson. I believe you."

"Arrr, you're both a kind and a wise man." He sat back down at the table.

"So, is there a story in the harpoon or the metal plate?"

"Not much of a story in either one. The harpoon were just one of those freak accidents that happens when you're swimming with ten sharks during a feeding frenzy. It's really not much of a story at all—at least not much of a story worthy of a fine piece o' pie."

"You swam with ten sharks during a feeding frenzy?"

"Aye, but they're fast! Very hard to catch with your hands. You need a harpoon or some very good luck."

"You swam with sharks while they were having a feeding frenzy and you tried to catch one? That's hard to believe."

"It weren't the sharks having the feeding frenzy; it were the sailors. You see, we ran out of rations a week-and-a-half before. We were hungry. Hungry like a school of snappers. Ya had to sleep with one eye open for fear that one of the others might be as hungry as you, if you knows what I mean."

"When we saw the sharks, five of us jumped in, with twenty more egging us on. There was one Brian Jensen, a green-horn landlubber, on his first voyage. He was the fool with the harpoon. But it didn't turn out all bad. With the blood in the water, we caught us enough to feed the crew for two months.

"That's where I really learned to love the taste of shark. I love shark steaks, shark-fin soup, shark-tail kabob, shark-liver patté, shark-eye pudding, shark omelet and shark strüdel. I'll tell ya, if it's made with shark, I loves it! Ya see, shark is a white meat—chewy, you bet— but delightfully filling." He had a distant, happy look in his eyes and a hint of a smile on one side of his mouth."

The waitress brought us our meals. Bob began a feeding frenzy of his own. He used both hands, not bothering himself with any utensils.

"How did you lose your boat, Captain Bob Timpson?"

"You, my friend, are showing your land-it-tude-ness. That's 'land-it-tude-ness'." He pronounced it very slowly, then smiled at the word (which I felt he must have made up himself, or which was a word only used among the seamen). He quit smiling and became deadly serious. "A ship she were, the *Ocean Bloom*, a beautiful, fair and magnificent ship."

He ate two more bites of his shark, then looked sternly at me as he spoke. "There be times and places in the ocean when and where the sea-wise sailors will not travel. There are times when the sea, she will warn you. 'Red sky at night, sailor delight; red in the morning, sailors take warning.' You knows, I lost me ship, but that's not all. With her went me crew—every last one."

"When I awoke that fateful morning, the sky, she were as red as the petals of a rose on Valentine's Day. I called to the crew to wake them. We all knew that the storm, she would be bad, but no one knew how bad and angry she would be. We went to our posts. We dropped the sails and we tightened down everything we could on top and on the bottom."

"It was calm at first—too calm. We watched the sky blacken and the storm clouds come towards us. The wind blew and hit us hard from the east. We tried to outrun her, but she soon had us in her bosom and would not let us go. With full power we headed straight east into her heart, hoping to fight through her sooner. She was blowing us backwards faster than the engines at full throttle could move us forward. Waves at first were twenty feet, then they grew: thirty, forty, fifty—some swells as high as a hundred feet from crest to trough!"

"Lightning was not only striking all around us, it was hitting our masts, our railings and everything on deck. Every time the lighting struck the ship, the plate in my head and the harpoon point in my west end would spark and vibrate."

"But the storm, she didn't take us. She blew us a thousand miles off-course, but didn't take us. She tried, but we rode her. Everything she threw at us, the *Ocean Bloom* took. She were strong. I were sure the lightning or the waves or the wind would put us under, but they didn't—and oh that they would have—for ya see, the storm, she took us to where no man should ever go. A place no man should ever see. She took us to the edge of the ocean. Not the edge that separates land from water, but the edge that separates this world from Eternity. Here you can not only see the stars and the cosmos above you, but below you, as well. There the *Ocean Bloom* floated in air! It must have been air, for there were no water or land above or below us."

"It were here where all the scurviest dragons, monsters, giant serpents and the visions from your nightmares go when they're no longer needed on Earth. Monsters! Thousands upon thousands of monsters. Eyes as big as wagon wheels. At first they didn't see us, then a big one with fiery red eyes looked directly at us and started to snap and lunge. The men fired their weapons. Aye, but that were a mistake, for the rest of the creatures awoke and leaped and flew and clawed at us."

"Some men fought the beasts, while others raised and set the sails. I held the wheel. Thousands of hideous monsters! Millions of razor-sharp fangs and claws—every one of them striking and gnashing and trying to make us their meal. Every instant we knew would be our last, but we would not go down without a fight! We would not surrender to our fears. We would not fail without hurling all of our strength in the cause of life."

"My only wantings were to return to the ocean and take our chances against that storm. Against that she-devil. My men were brave and never quit—no not one. Only that such bravery could be rewarded. . . ."

His voice trailed off and it seemed to me that his heart and mind were in another time and place. There was a long pause.

"Is that where you lost your *Ocean Bloom*?" I asked, after I could wait no longer—hoping he would finish his story.

"Arrr, no, it weren't. Ya sees, we made it back to the ocean, we did. Mind you, it were never easy, but we made it back. Fighting the beasts and the ocean, the wind, the waves and the currents. We made it back to Newport, where the bank, that monster's mother-in-law, she took me ship!"

"A bank took your ship?"

"Arrr, it seems I were a mere fourteen years behind on me payments."

"So the bank took your ship?"

"Aye."

"What about your crew?"

"It's hard to keep a crew without a boat."

"You mean ship."

"Arrr, I guess me do."

He finished his dinner and with a story like

that, I bought him the biggest piece of blackberry pie they had. He ate it, nearly in one bite.

"And now ya knows me story," he said as he smiled and touched the side of his nose and was gone. I was looking right at him when he disappeared. It startled me. I quickly looked under the table, but he wasn't there. He had completely vanished. On the chair, where he was sitting, was piled his dinner—with nearly a whole piece of pie on top.

I stood there looking at the chair in amazement when the waitress came.

"I hate when he comes in," she said. "He always makes such a mess."

LETTER FROM THE AUTHOR

Now that you have met the Pirates of *Pirates, Ghosts and Zombies*, come and meet the rest. Of course you know there are Ghosts and Zombies, but what you don't know is, among the rest of the cast, there are Comedians, Travel Agents, Aliens, Authors, Snooty English Professors and the Grim Reaper. In *Pirates, Ghosts, Zombies* you'll find an eclectic catch of characters who I am sure you would love to invite into your home and get to know a little better.

Thanks,

Mark

P.S. For a great read, don't forget, *Rabbitman II the Second of Scott, Scott III the Third Tale of Rabbitman* and *Bizarre but True Tales from the Twenty-Third Dimension*.

P.S.S. When you think about it, stop by amazon.com and buy a copy of *KOSMIC KARL*, it's a low budget independently produced film. I wrote and directed it. Buy a copy for your mother too. (Starving actors and the crew will join me in thanking you).

Come visit us at www.iawriters.com for other books, short stories and films.

SPECIAL THANKS

To succeed as a writer, one must have a lot of support and I would like to thank a few of those people who has made it possible for me. My parents, who are great, my family (brothers, sisters, wife and kids), plus Paul Drake (who is my nephew, who did the art for this book). I would also like to thank Cindy Whipple for making the final edit of this book. If you see any mistakes, you can blame them on her. Additional thanks go to Garron Bently and Randy Chatwin (two life-long friends and inspirations).

However my biggest thanks must to go to my little brother, Gary Whipple of IA Writers. He is amazing. He has taken my writings from a drawer in a filing cabinet, where they would have stayed, perhaps forever, proof read, edited and published them. He's amazing. Together, we made a little film, *Kosmic Karl*, with a host of talented people. It was fun and wonderful until we found that our constant speed film camera was defective. Instead of running at 24 frames per second, it fluctuated between, 18 and 30 fps. depending on the charge of the battery. Sound synchronization for film is tough and time consuming when everything is working right. He had to re-sync the sound to the film every three seconds of the entire film. Without him, *Kosmic Karl* would only be a dream/nightmare and would only be a bunch of unedited un-synced rolls of film collecting dust in the bottom of my closet.

ABOUT THE AUTHOR

Mark Whipple is a film director, screenwriter, novelist, philanthropist (gave his favorite bowling ball to charity), song writer, writer for the stage, an all-around nice guy who loves the short story, (reading or writing) and an inter-galactic — inter-dimensional space historian, (as we find in the Rabbitman trilogy and Bizarre but True Tales from the Twenty-Third Dimension). His hobbies include: boomerang making and tossing, skiing, boating and car racing (pinewood derby variety—He once took first place, in both the Fathers of the Boys - No Rules Race, and first place in the Hottest Chili Beans Contest…in the same day).

His loves include his lovely wife Joni of 24-plus years, his wonderful, brilliant and beautiful children and a pick-up basketball game. Although he fears heights, Mark likes spending his spare time on roofs—he finds the air and the view fresher there. He likes pets, i.e. cats, dogs, iguana, head lice (I'm sorry, he said he doesn't like head lice—and one must point out that he has owned cats, dogs and one iguana, but has never had head lice, but still believes that he would not like them).

Mark Whipple was born in 1960, in Salt Lake City, Utah, to well behaved parents. He is the eighth of nine children. As he thinks about it, his family mainly consists of artists: potters, jewelers, painters, cartoonists, singers and editors (film and print). Each are amazing and gifted in their own way. (But things weren't always so happy in the family, he has an older sister who could beat up any boy in the neighborhood—who didn't let her talents go idle when there were no neighbor boys around—she could beat up all of her three younger and smaller brothers at once...major embarrassment to the boys.)

Mark has attended various schools, including: Onequa Elementary, Glendale Jr High, West High School and the University of Utah. Of the four schools, Mark was sent to the principal's office and expelled the fewest times in the last one. (However this may be a trick answer since the University of Utah doesn't have a principal.)

Concerning his upbringing, Mark has often said "I never minded wearing my brother's hand-me-downs, I only wish my mother didn't have his shoes bronzed".

In 1984, Mark had finished his fourth screenplay, SPIKE, IKE AND FIFTYTOES, it is a story of a bunch of ghosts who are tired of being dead, so they decide to get their old band back together. The screenplay landed him his first Hollywood agent. The agent told Mark that this screenplay was an "Overnight seller." Upon clarification of the term "Overnight", the agent promised to have it sold in three months. So while Mark waited for the overnight sale to happen, he continued to write and write—throw boomerangs, and write. He has written three novels, two collections of short stories, one and a half stage plays, twenty-nine feature length screenplays, (one of which, Kosmic Karl, he filmed) and a few songs—some of the songs are featured in Kosmic Karl. He has also thrown countless boomerangs 173,562 times.

Mark loves life, the opportunities and challenges which he always faces with hope and humor. Applications for royalty in his fan club are now being accepted.

www.iawriters.com

19346394R00131

Made in the USA
San Bernardino, CA
22 February 2015